Love and Death in the Valley:

Awakening to Hidden Histories and Forgotten Crimes on the West Coast of Canada

by

Rev. Kevin D. Annett
author of "Hidden from History: The Canadian Holocaust"
(2001)

© 2002 by Kevin Annett. All rights reserved.

No part of this book may be reproduced, stored in a retrieval system, or transmitted by any means, electronic, mechanical, photocopying, recording, or otherwise, without written permission from the author.

ISBN: 1-4033-4819-7 (e-book)
ISBN: 1-4033-4820-0 (Paperback)

This book is printed on acid free paper.

Contents

Preface v

Foreword vii

Chapter One: Snapshots of Heaven 1

Chapter Two: Land-Grabs and Empty Stomachs, or A Tale of Two Letters 37

Chapter Three: Learning to Speak the Unspeakable—A Funeral, An Inquisition and a Tribunal 62

Chapter Four: Meanwhile, Back on Campus: Sabotage and Intrigue in the Hallowed Halls of Learning 115

Interlude: On Fear and its Children, and other Banalities 128

Chapter Five: What Cannot be Healed, or Spoken: After the Inquisition 134

Interlude: By Way of a Reflection—On Saints, Ministers, and other Strange Persons 154

Chapter Six: An Unfinished Story, or Now What Will You Do? ... 160

Author's Note: 179

About the Author 181

Preface

This is a book which every North American needs to read.

At this very moment, the lands of the aboriginal people of north-central British Columbia are being flooded and destroyed by corporations like the North American Water and Power Alliance, and compliant Indian politicians who are evicting their own people from their land. Canada's water and hydro-electric power is destined for America, if the Canadian government and their masters in Washington have their way.

Once again, the poorest of native people are being sacrificed in a massive land grab. And the water you will drink tomorrow will be tainted with their blood.

This is the face of Genocide in Canada today: a slaughter which began long ago and has never stopped, merely changed its image.

As I am so often told by native survivors in healing circles and ceremonies, everything boils down to the land and its resources, and who owns them. And this is the core issue behind everything that you will read in my book.

That makes this a very compelling, and relevant story for all North Americans. For if Genocide can happen to Indian people today, it can happen to you tomorrow – especially if you rely on the very government and corporate system that has robbed and murdered them for so long.

What you will discover in this book may shock and horrify you, or it may confirm what you already know about our world: especially if you are an aboriginal person and somehow survived the nightmare of "residential school". But either way, this is a story about the future of all of us, native or not.

"Love and Death in the Valley" is a very personal story, about the re-education of a "white" minister by the facts of Genocide all around him. And it is also a story that keeps getting bigger, as one revelation of unspeakable crimes has opened up yet another Pandora's Box of torture, death, and corruption at the highest levels of power on our continent.

And yet ultimately, this is a story of great hope and survival, of how it's possible to be courageous when it matters.

The world may be crazy with injustice, but you and I don't have to be.

Rev. Kevin D. Annett
1 September, 2002

"…what has happened to him is outrageous."

Dr. Noam Chomsky
7 August, 2002, referring to
Rev. Kevin Annett

Foreword

I've had the kind of experience that most people dread: being quickly and brutally stripped of one's job, livelihood, family and reputation by a handful of unaccountable men.

From the top of the hill, if you like, I was tossed down into a garbage heap. In a few months, I went from being a comfortable clergyman to a penniless ex-minister shunned by colleagues and friends alike. I was once a happy family man who revelled each morning in the joy of my two young daughters; suddenly, I saw my children only on occasion, snatching what bits of normalcy was allowed by divorce and "access hours".

My life was ruined in this way because I offended a group of powerful and wealthy people.

As a minister, I tried to be what I thought a Christian was: a sanctuary for the lonely and the impoverished. I opened my church and my pulpit to aboriginal survivors of my church's notorious "residential schools", and from there these men and women spoke of murders and other hidden crimes by officials of those schools. And I discovered that my church was selling off native ancestral land to its corporate benefactors for considerable money, and covering the whole thing up.

I did not remain silent about these wrongs, since that would have made me an accomplice in them. For such fidelity to my ordination vows and my integrity as a man, I have been mercilessly punished and terrorized by officials of the United Church of Canada and their friends in government and big business, who are criminally implicated in what I inadvertently exposed.

This nightmare burst upon my unsuspecting life in the new year of 1995, in the small logging town of Port Alberni on Canada's west coast, where I was a minister of the United Church. Nothing has ever been the same for me since January 23, 1995, when I was summarily fired and prevented from working again in the church to which I had devoted my life.

In one sense, the nightmare only worsened after my expulsion, as my marriage collapsed, I lost my children in a terrible custody battle, and I fell into poverty after the United Church officialdom permanently expelled me from the ministry without once charging me with anything. And yet these trials caused me to discover my true self by being stripped of everything but myself, like a man who has suffered and died, and then come back from hell with a new mind and heart—and an incredible story to share.

Ultimately, this story is not simply about a whistle-blowing clergyman who was crushed by his own church; it's about the numerically biggest crime in human history—the extermination of more than eighty million aboriginal people on our continent by European Christianity. My story is a snapshot of what happened when a minister of that religion was forced to face its actual legacy, up close, in hungry and dying people, and ask himself whether such a religion was worth believing in anymore.

Like some of the survivors of church and state-sponsored Genocide whom you will meet in this book, I have recovered from my brutalization even while carrying its scars. Step by step, a mystery has led me back into my centre once more, and into the place where I am to be: a pulpit, a restored family, and a high place from which to tell a disbelieving world about the "hidden holocaust" my culture and religion inflicted on indigenous Canadians.

And yet, on Sunday mornings in my Port Alberni church, I never insisted that people believe what I said. I always urged them to figure things out for themselves, especially the most important matters: of love, and God, and how we put all the nice words into practice in our own backyard.

I ask the same thing of the reader. I hope my story will help you do so. But know that it is a tale born of my suffering, and loss, and endless nights—and the pain of so many aboriginal people who have not spoken and can never speak.

I dedicate this book to them; and also to my wife Pamela, and my daughters Clare and Elinor, for whom I have struggled, and without whom I could not have.

Kevin Daniel Annett
on the seventh anniversary of my firing
January 23, 2002
Vancouver, Canada

<u>Chapter One:</u> **Snapshots of Heaven**

Where sympathy is renewed, life is restored.
   Vincent van Gogh

Cecilia Joseph had a perfect view of the Alberni inlet as she choked to death.

Her soul, like the smoke from her slum apartment fire, hung gently over the valley her ancestors had inhabited for millennia, unhurried as it followed the wind's meandering up the Somass river, like the salmon that struggle and mostly die there every fall. But Cecilia's spirit, like her tortured life, found no rest, even among the quiet cedar trees. It stabbed towards heaven: a single, bleeding question mark.

Her eyes impaled me with the same punctuation whenever she helped me bag groceries for other hungry people at my church food bank: always the same "why?", dripping from her like sap off a split trunk. I could not answer her at the time, for I didn't even understand her question. But I've been looking for an answer ever since she was cremated alive on September 5, 1995, because there was no handle on her apartment door, and no escape.

The exits are bolted shut on her people, not by accident; and the fires which are killing so many of them are being deliberately set. Trapped in a burning barn, locked in by faceless men, left to choke alone in a million hidden places.

Sometimes, these unfortunates stumble out of the ashes and carry what's left of themselves along the roadside, scrounging for life, asking for help. And sometimes they come to church, of all places.

That's where I first met Cecilia Joseph; not during a hymn, but in the basement of St. Andrew's United Church, in a food bank line, where she belonged. For if Mohandas Gandhi was right, and *"God dare not appear to the hungry except as bread"*, then Cecilia had no need to be upstairs, among the cushioned pews where God is imagined between belches. There was no place for her there, anyway; all the seats were reserved.

Like in the early Roman catacombs, God took flesh in the basement and dwelled among the nameless, that deep winter of 1993.

....

They should make excellent slaves, since it appears that they have no religion whatsoever.
Christopher Columbus, on his first contact with New World aboriginals, 1493

My part in this story began on a cold morning in March of 1992, when I drove for the first time into the Alberni Valley on Vancouver Island. From the highway summit of Mount Arrowsmith, marked by a few still-uncut towering cedar trees, I saw a land ringed by coastal mountains, falling away to the distant Pacific shore. But the land was buried in an impenetrable fog that morning, which draped over the valley even in broad daylight.

As I plunged into that cloud I felt that I had entered an even deeper fog, where ghosts walked, and secrets remained hidden.

Nothing was clear, at first, besides the fact that I was bound for a job interview at St. Andrew's United Church: a score of mostly retired white loggers and mill workers who yearned for more numbers in their pews; yearned, more honestly, for a return to the clearer times of filled churches and zero unemployment and segregated ferries with the Indians safely shoved below decks. And ten sober but desperate faces studied me to see if I would restore such good times to their shrinking congregation, as their new minister.

A dying mill town isn't the place where one expects things to change very much, except for the worse. Besides, my notion of change quickly went beyond simply rebuilding my parish. The poverty in town and on the local Indian reserves was appalling.

The same year I arrived there, Port Alberni was ranked by the provincial government as the second poorest community in British Columbia, the town with the highest level of infant mortality and family violence, and the suicide capital of the west coast. And at the bottom of this heap of suffering were the local Indian nations: one third of the population perched on not even one percent of the land that had once been theirs.

Love and Death in the Valley

I didn't know it when I drove so blindly into that valley, but I had stumbled on the scene of a mass murder: the centre of the west coast Christian missionary invasion that had killed off 99 of every 100 native people in barely two generations, during the smallpox epidemics of the mid-1800's.

The Port Alberni Indians are the remnants of this conquest, and continue to die from it in droves. But it remains an invisible slaughter to most of us. For all I saw that first morning were ten pale, polite faces, and a quiet, tree-lined neighbourhood.

They were familiar faces to me. I had been raised around people like them, being a child of the United Church and its Scottish Presbyterianism: serious and straight-laced souls embodying what writer Pierre Berton describes as the English-Canadian mixed personality: one with the mind of a Scottish banker and the heart of a Gaelic mystic, and completely unsure of who to be.

So I understood the confusion of the men and women who interviewed and then unanimously chose me as their new minister, and what moved them: their desire to run a church more orderly than joyous, their innate generosity hamstrung by a fear of the stranger, and their deep and sullen guilt at dwelling on the bones of another people, having once been the conquered themselves, back in northern Ireland and Scotland.

And yet, for all their familiarity, the St. Andrew's remnant seemed odd to me, like how I imagined the Afrikaner Boers or Ulster Protestants to be: a people who feel besieged.

There isn't much that doesn't threaten the pale folks of Port Alberni: ghosts of Indian children from the past, more layoffs at the pulp mill from the future, and hordes of young environmental protesters from the present. And over it all sits the local feudal lord, the American logging corporation Weyerhauser—formerly MacMillan-Bloedel, when I arrived—which holds all the strings of power in town; including, I learned the hard way, in the church.

Somewhere in the midst of these fears, my new employers had circled their wagons and invited me to be the pastor of their snug little fortress. From their gun-slit perspective, my task was straightforward: to know who to let into their select circle, while comforting and protecting them from all of the threats outside: past, present and future.

This was euphemistically called "being pastorally competent" in the gray fraternity of my fellow clergy. But exactly where God, the Gospels and the rest of humanity fit into it all was never mentioned. I discovered why very quickly.

It wasn't something I set out to discover. I was content, at first, to be the kept chaplain on that luxury boat, for my life had been stormy with political activism, and I longed for days not filled with the suffering of others, with unwinnable causes and unbeatable foes. I saw myself settling down in Port Alberni with my wife of that time and our young two daughters, and having what our pig-sty impulses call "a normal life". I wanted bits of other people and their problems, an arms-length god who causes nice feelings but not anguish. I wanted to preach good sermons.

And it all would have happened, except for a fatal "flaw". I retained a smattering of empathy that kept my door open just enough to allow in a few, initial strangers who would pry me open even more, and eventually change me.

I neither wanted nor anticipated to be changed so. I had become your typical minister, trained in the art of partial gestures, ready and able to hand a bag of groceries to a starving woman and feel fine about it all. Until I, too, began to hunger.

This transformation began my first week on the job at St. Andrew's. My inaugural sermon had been pleasantly received with a sort of terminal niceness by the handful of old-timers in the pews. Innocently, I asked one of them over tea after the service why there were no native people in church, when most of them in the area had been baptised as United Church members.

Nicety suddenly vanished like a cedar tree before chain saws. The old fellow nearly coughed on his cookie. He turned quite red, and sputtered, "They don't want anything to do with us. We've tried, but they're totally unreasonable. You'd better leave them to themselves, Kevin."

That perked my curiosity more than anything, and so it was with near relief that I received my first phone call from a native person the next week.

He was an elderly man named Danny Gus of the Tseshaht Indian band west of town, and he wanted to get married. I drove out to the reserve that same day, and entered a new world.

Love and Death in the Valley

Danny and Clothilda had been living together for forty years, and now that their grandchildren were appearing they wanted to tie the knot.

"It's the right thing to do, we figure" Danny told me, over tea and chummis, which is salmon eggs in oil, and tastes as bad as it sounds. "We said we'd never do it, but there's the kids to consider. Setting them a good example. You know."

Danny moved his tired fisherman's body and stared out the window. He was looking at the nearby school yard. I didn't know then that the United Church's Alberni Indian Residential School had once stood there.

I had learned from working with native people on Vancouver's skid row that it was impolite to ask too many questions. I had to be invited to listen to someone's story. So I waited, while Clothilda made more tea and Danny gazed out at the school yard.

"We never go to church" Danny finally muttered. He looked at me with somber brown eyes that were trying to explain so much.

I was about to say something when he continued, "I saw some bad things in that residential school. Things I've never told anybody."

"Why didn't you tell anyone?" I asked. He looked at me like I was stupid, or six years old.

"Who could I tell? They killed kids there. They buried them in secret, in those hills out back. Friends of mine. It happened all the time. The church people know all about it, and they're scared of us. They don't want us in their church."

I began visiting more Indian homes after that, whenever I could. Because I never asked people to come to church and I wasn't pushing religion on them, I was accepted and even trusted in the hovels and slum apartments where most of the Tseshahts and Ahousahts and other local Indians live.

The nightmare began to be shared with me.

I heard of children being raped and killed by clergy, and unspeakably tortured at the residential school where the law forced every Indian child to attend. I was told of pedophile rings that still operated, of Indian leaders dealing drugs and exploiting their own children. I saw seven children huddled in one unheated room and living for weeks on noodles. I began presiding at funerals, most of

5

them of children, or teenagers who had killed themselves. I learned very quickly that any Indian is expendable, like any poor person.

Within a few months of my arrival, I had opened a food bank in the church basement because of the army of hungry families in town. Amazingly enough, there was no food bank in Port Alberni until we opened ours. A native woman, Debbie Seward, came up with the name "Loaves and Fishes" for it, and sure enough miracles began happening, the kind that can only be witnessed and never described.

But I did try to preach about it, especially when the hungry began walking upstairs to church services on Sundays. A living sermon started to play itself out in the formerly empty pews of St. Andrew's United Church.

Perhaps it was, more accurately, a passion play, in which the soul of a person or a whole people—in this case, a church—is fought over by light and darkness. Where great issues and stakes are wrestled out in the realm of individuals' consciences and deeds. Where people are tested, and sifted, according to an unknown script, and some hidden playwright.

There is a funny moment in the Bible when Jesus is being baptised on the banks of the Jordan River. Quite the religious revival is going on all around Christ, so much so that no-one seems to realise who he is. The baptism industry is so busy churning out the saved that everyone misses that all the religion is just a prop, a setting of the stage, for the important event, which is that God is actually making an appearance in a stale little backwater.

That's what seemed to be happening in St. Andrew's, the more that haggard strangers began coming to church. Something of God made itself known, which is why I can't really describe what took place.

Although I must try to tell this story, doing so is like the same lonely incompleteness that I felt each Sunday in my pulpit, when I tried to speak of the wonder in our midst, what some natives call The Great Mystery. Or, like when I was ten years old, and I ran in from a sudden prairie thunderstorm, drenched with radiance, and I tried to tell my father of the joy in my every pore. All I could say to him was "Come on Dad!". But he would never join me in the rain.

We are alone in our ecstasy, and in our truth, and we must learn how to remain alone in both if we are to survive the pain of it all and

Love and Death in the Valley

not die to our dreams. For how many times have we learned, too sadly, that the golden moments cannot be repeated: fathers leave, children die, messiahs are murdered, and the clarity that makes sense of everything for a moment gets shovelled under mountains of dung. But how to tell my congregants that hard news, as they stand, so hopefully, to catch and hold God in a bit of communion bread, final and secure?

Trying to make sense of the suffering and the beauty swirling around me in Port Alberni every day sharpened me to the truth of such limitations, and yet also to the possibility of transcending them, of being able to make a difference despite everything that's arrayed against us. What made change possible for me was seeing it happen around me in others.

A Mexican priest named Javier who was later murdered by a landowner's death squad told me something once that haunts me, and which was borne out during my ministry in Port Alberni:

"The poor have only one hope: a new world. And the rich have only one fear: a new world."

Allowing a new world to take shape and live through you can be pretty dangerous, for it offends the comfortable; and yet absolutely necessary, for it gives life to the destitute. I found that I had to choose ten times a day whether to risk offending or angering the former in order to serve the latter.

Such a test came my way soon after the food bank crowd began attending my church.

One Sunday in the spring of 1993, a young native woman named Karen Connerley came to church with her kids, Eric and Kendra. The three of them lived in one of the slum apartments in the "ghetto" part of town, as they called it, and I had got to know them well. Karen's eldest child, a baby named Charlie junior, had died of pneumonia in their unheated fleabag the same year. Karen carried her grief like she bore her other children: with an angry dignity that tolerated nothing less than understanding of her plight, and action to help her children.

The pale folks in church that day didn't seem to care about sympathising with Karen or her kids, who were running around the sanctuary in the delight of finally being out of their cramped apartment. Karen, Indian style, expected others to take a hand in managing her kids, while the matrons of St. Andrew's wondered aloud, and indignantly, why Karen didn't discipline her own "brats".

Things came to a head during prayer time. Six year old Eric didn't want to leave with the other kids, and he started crying as soon as I began to pray aloud.

I tried incorporating his wails into my words, actually, and I remember saying thanks to God for the cries of children so that we didn't forget their empty stomachs. But that didn't work for some of the church ladies, who stormed up to me after the service.

"Either she leaves or we do!" thundered one of them, whose name I forget. "You'll have to ask her to go".

Other, non-native children had often cried during our services, and this irate woman had never seemed to mind. But an Indian child was another matter. I told the woman that I wasn't going to evict anyone from the church, and I encouraged her to work it out with Karen. Wrong answer, it seems, for the matron left and never returned.

Just like the following year, when I was asked by three "influential" board members to close our food bank for the sake of "congregational harmony", I faced a simple choice that Sunday morning. It wasn't the obvious one, of deciding between a rich woman and a poor woman. For me, it boiled down to whether I would actually practice what I preached.

Clergy aren't expected to do so, of course, and most of us don't. Practising what you advocate from a pulpit can get you in deep trouble, and doesn't do much for "congregational harmony". And while I could have carried on for years at St. Andrew's by sticking to nice sentiments and allowing the old guard to evict Indians and other newcomers from the church at will, I wouldn't have seen much when I looked into the mirror every morning.

One such test wasn't enough, it seems, for they began to come fast and furious as the newcomers stayed in church. Their very presence each Sunday was a rush of Port Alberni reality spilling into our little sanctuary.

During our worship time, environmentalists found themselves perched next to loggers; Indian welfare moms mingled with businessmen at coffee hour. And, after the initial illusion of oneness had given way to the real differences between us, niceness changed

Love and Death in the Valley

into what the founder of Methodism, John Wesley, liked to call "God's Good Trouble". The truth stood up and spoke, of all places, in a church. And it was not "nice".

Take World Food Sunday, for instance. It's supposed to be a time every October when United Church congregations focus on hunger in the world; always, of course, from a safe distance. Prayers are said for Guatemalans, or Tanzanians, and funds are sent to some sad-eyed kid in Malawi. The more "radical" congregations may even ship off parcels to the local food bank. But the reality of hunger is kept confined, like God, to a notice on the church bulletin.

All of that went out the window of our church on October 14, 1993.

By that time, after more than a year at St. Andrew's, I had been opening up my pulpit every Sunday to anyone who wanted to speak. I thought this was even more appropriate to do on that World Food Sunday, since by then there were many people in the congregation who used our Loaves and Fishes food bank to survive every month.

But none of us expected the words of Jenny Munn, a young mother on welfare.

Jenny strode to the pulpit like Jesus must have when he was about to trash the money changers. She gripped its edges and barked at the congregation, "We're saying all these nice words about hunger today when there's lots of people in our own town who have nothing. I haven't been able to feed my own kids for weeks. I can't believe how uncaring you all are. You just go about your comfortable lives and don't see the suffering at your own doorstep. Do any of you give a shit about me, or my kids?

"It's time we got justice, not more charity. I don't care about your food bank. The time is coming when we're going to take what's ours, not beg for it. Think of all the millions of dollars in logs MacMillan-Bloedel is hauling out of this valley every day, and a third of us in Alberni are poor.

"If we're going to do anything besides talk we'd better start changing our own community, getting rid of all these differences in wealth. If Jesus was here today he'd be saying the same thing. And he'd get crucified for it again. Well, you can't crucify all of us. You can't crucify the truth. And I'm not going to rest until all the kids in this valley have enough to eat."

Some of the congregation broke into applause: native families, and members of LIFT—Low Income Folks Together, our local anti-poverty group. But before Jenny had sat down a long-time member of the church who would later help have me fired, Shirley Whyte, hurried up to the pulpit. Equal time, I thought.

"I'm sick and tired of our worship hour being used to attack me and other well-off members of the church, and make us feel guilty for having money. I'm a good Christian. I've worked hard for people in this community and I'm not going to be criticised in my own church by some…".

Shirley stopped suddenly and glared at me like I was a cockroach. Then she stormed back to her seat, to murmurs of approval and a few boos.

I asked both Jenny and Shirley to help me serve communion that morning in the service, but only Jenny responded. The frail woman stood with me at the front of the church as everyone lined up for the bread and the juice.

Danny Gus, who had first told me of the murders at the Alberni residential school, was there that morning, along with his wife Clothilda. He took my hand as the two of them approached me and whispered, "We were never allowed to take communion with white people in this town. No church would have us. Thank you from all of us."

Danny and Clothilda were crying as they returned to their seats, as was Omma van Beek, the oldest member of our congregation. A widow for decades, Omma had come from Holland after the war and was one of the "silent majority" in the church: always in her pew, never involved in disputes, struggling to remain alert and mobile at ninety-two. Omma always cried during communion, and I took her thin hand in mine as I brought her the communion elements.

"This is the body of our saviour, broken for you, Omma" I said to her. She looked at me through her tears, across a weary lifetime, and said something to me in Dutch with a smile like a newborn's.

The knot of pale families who had run St. Andrew's for generations—I call them the Old Guard—tended to sit together at the back of the church, as if to monitor all that was happening. They were thus clustered that Sunday, and as I approached with communion they hurried out the back door of the sanctuary like frightened moles.

I looked to the front of the church just then, to check on how Jenny was doing with communion, and a throng of people were gathered around the table sharing out what remained of the loaf. To some, I thought, it is all so natural; to others, merely a threat. But the truth was there for all of us to see. All were invited to the great sharing, but only some actually came: the ones who hungered and knew that they did. And not simply the well-fed, but the guilty went away empty.

I felt innumerable spirits breathe a sigh of happy release when this Good Trouble appeared in our congregation, for it was like a key turning in the closed door that was Port Alberni, and its century or more of secret crimes.

Through the fissures of the conflict that was bubbling forth each Sunday began to sound the voices of long-buried people and truths. But little did I know how hideous were the crimes, and how terrible the cries.

....

When the European missionaries came, we had the land and they had the Bible. Now we have the Bible and they have the land.
Desmond Tutu, Archbishop of South Africa.

We couldn't begin to investigate all the deaths of children at the Alberni residential school. It would be too huge an investigation.
Constable Gerry Peters, RCMP, October 3, 1997

Harriett Nahanee's real name is Tsebeoilt, of the Pacheedaht Nation on Vancouver Island. She was never part of my congregation in Port Alberni, but she spent five years as a child in the United Church residential school in the same town. She was kidnapped at the age of ten from her ancestral village of Clo-ose near Port Renfrew, on Vancouver Island's rugged west coast, and was brought to the school by people she calls "terrorists in uniform": RCMP officers. And there, on Christmas eve in 1946, she witnessed a murder.

It wasn't an unusual death, for Indian children were regularly killed in the residential schools, especially in Port Alberni. Nor was its concealment for fifty years odd, since more than 50,000 young corpses have somehow gone missing from the residential school records.

What was different about the murder of fourteen year old Maisie Shaw by Reverend Alfred Caldwell was that it was the first such crime ever publicly reported in the mainstream press in British Columbia, and it led to the first attempt to seriously investigate crimes of Genocide committed in Canadian residential schools.

"Genocide" is an antiseptic word that doesn't begin to describe the horror, and magnitude, of the greatest mass murder in human history: the extermination of New World indigenous peoples by Christianity. Nearly one hundred million corpses lie between the time of Christopher Columbus and Maisie Shaw. Of Maisie's own ancestors, over 98% of them had died from smallpox and other European diseases by the time she was kidnapped, along with Tsebeoilt and whole villages of children, and imprisoned in the Alberni "residential school".

It wasn't a "school", first of all. It was a death camp, designed to kill off the majority of Indian children while training a handful of native collaborators who would one day faithfully serve land-grabbing corporations and treaty-seeking governments.

Most of the children in these "schools" never went to classes. Those who survived deliberate exposure to tuberculosis, and starvation, and beatings, were put to work in the fields and kitchen, or farmed out to wealthy pedophiles, or used as human guinea pigs by pharmaceutical companies in their drug testing programs. Many of them were sexually sterilised by church doctors, in hospitals run by churches and the federal government. **And nearly one-half of them died in the residential schools.**

Tsebeoilt was one of the "lucky" ones. She was raped almost every day of her life for five years by Principal Caldwell, Edward Peake and other male staff, she went without food, and had her teeth regularly operated on without painkillers. But she survived.

One of the ways she did so was by hiding from her torturers. It was from such a shelter, under the basement stairs of the girls' dormitory at the Alberni residential school, that Harriett saw Principal Caldwell murder Maisie Shaw on the evening of December 24, 1946.

Love and Death in the Valley

I was at the bottom of the stairs in the basement. I heard her crying, she was looking for her mother. Then I heard Caldwell kick her and she fell down the stairs. I went to look—her eyes were open, she wasn't moving. I never saw her again.

("Claim of Murder Goes Back to '40's", The Vancouver Sun, Dec. 18, 1995)

Alfred Caldwell died in bed, not in prison, or on a cold basement floor, like his young victim. His crime was quickly covered up by the United Church in British Columbia, whose officials told Maisie's parents that their daughter had been killed by a train. Not bothering to coordinate their lies with the church, the RCMP claimed that in fact Maisie had died of pneumonia, a story they continue to uphold, even though funeral home and cemetery records flatly contradict their claim.

I didn't know about Maisie Shaw when I ministered just a mile from where she was murdered. Nor did I meet Tsebeoilt until a year after I was suddenly fired without cause from my pulpit after I allowed survivors of the residential school to speak from there. But the daughter of Maisie's murderer, Alfred Caldwell, was part of the Old Guard in my church, and she visibly winced whenever a native person stepped up to my pulpit to tell their story.

If I was ignorant of the crimes, and of the literal skeletons in the church's closet, there were others around me who were not: the very people who arranged my rapid removal from St. Andrew's, and who expelled me forever from United Church ministry in 1997.

What is another dead Indian child, in an ocean of corpses? Maisie's fate was the norm, not some perverse exception. Murderers like Alfred Caldwell acted with the full knowledge and consent of both church and state in our country, as part of a planned program of intentional genocide of Indians that was crafted in Ottawa in the fall of 1910.

All of this is on the public record, another fact I didn't know until I had been thrown out of the church, and I began a Ph.D. program at the University of British Columbia. That's where I stumbled across Department of Indian Affairs archives in a dank library basement that opened the lid on Genocide in our country.

We are talking about a Hidden Holocaust in Canada that is directly comparable to the Nazi extermination of European Jews, operating under the same kind of laws, racist moral climate, and system of institutionalized and legal murder.

No foreign armies ever conquered Canada and held war crimes trials where the planners and perpetrators of this genocide were brought before international justice. Consequently, Euro-Canadians have never had to acknowledge, let alone be punished for, their home grown Holocaust.

The institutions which ran this Holocaust are still intact; indeed, they are so-called "revered" bodies, and are financially maintained by every Canadian taxpayer. They are the United, Anglican, Presbyterian and Roman Catholic Churches, the RCMP, and every level of government in this country. <u>And under international law, they are all guilty of crimes against humanity.</u>

But here's the catch: they are still the ones in charge.

....

For whatever reason, during my time as a minister in Port Alberni I found myself discovering undeniable facts about my church and my culture that were horrible and not at all in agreement with the view of both that I had been raised with. But "facts have hard heads", to quote Lenin, and when faced with them we can either play the denial game or try to come to grips with a new truth.

That's what I've been struggling to do for years now, as my life has crashed to pieces around me. And if I've been able to come to some new truths, it is only because I've found myself spanning two different worlds ever since arriving in Port Alberni on that rainy March morning in 1992.

I often felt dizzy and confused at the end of a typical day in my Port Alberni ministry, as I tried to connect the two, very different worlds I was moving through. One moment I'd be having tea with an elderly pale woman in her comfortable home, where her biggest problem was her loneliness now that her children were all grown up. An hour later, I'd be standing over the corpse of yet another dead

Love and Death in the Valley

Indian baby who had starved or frozen to death in an unheated shack on the local reserve.

The two worlds weren't just a privileged "white" reality and a third-world "Indian" one: they were, rather, the "official", and the actual, truth.

I did my best to bring these worlds together in my church, and especially in the Sunday service. That was one of the reasons I learned so quickly about the brutal reality of the local residential school. But uniting the Two Worlds under one roof was like bringing explosive substances together in a very small place.

The volatility wasn't just in seating an Indian mother on welfare next to a retired logger who thinks natives are mostly drunks. What happens, more basically, when you try to house truth alongside the industry of official lies that runs so much of our lives, and thoughts? Can both survive in close proximity for long?

That was the foremost question in my mind each week as I wrote my sermon, and stood up to deliver it. I sensed that truth was trying to find a seat in my church sanctuary as much, perhaps more, than the natives and poor people who were arriving in greater numbers all the time. But how to give it room, and welcome it, with more than a token smile and an invitation to stay for coffee afterwards? How to make the truth a full-time member of our church with full voice and vote at all the meetings?

As it turned out, we couldn't. Truth is like somebody farting during prayer time. It's like the kid in school who loves to scratch his fingernails along the blackboard and drive everyone crazy. Truth hurts too much for those who have slept in the same bed as guile. And so the ones who are complicit don't tolerate the truth hanging around for very long. Regardless of what you hear nowadays, the United Church did not and does not want to hear the truth of its own history, and of itself. And the "whites" in my congregation were no exception.

What's occasionally upsetting for the church is that truth will nevertheless refuse to budge when it's politely asked to vacate the pew, like the old homeless men who sleep in the back rows of churches on Vancouver's skid row. Like these transient guys, the truth can become utterly stubborn and belligerent when asked to leave, and, quite beyond reason and niceness, tell everyone to go fuck themselves.

It can go even further than that, like the poor sometimes do, and start a riot that smashes up all the arrangements of big temples, brandishing a whip and calling the church crowd all sorts of nasty names. And then, like the poor, it ends up on a cross, and the crucifiers make up stories to justify their bloody deed and blame the crucified for their own murder.

A brief history of Christianity, perhaps, but most definitely an encapsulation of what went on at my church during those exciting years when the Ghosts of Port Alberni began to walk and be heard.

To begin at the beginning, I need to take you back to a scene during my first months at St. Andrew's which lays out the actors, and the issues, in this story of Two Worlds in collision.

In a way, the scene was oddly like an episode in the film "Mister Smith Goes to Washington", when the naive young senator tries to introduce a bill for a kids' summer camp without knowing that the land he's trying to secure is essential to an expensive graft and speculation deal involving senior senators and their wealthy, secret funders. And then, of course, the shit hits the fan, especially for the neophyte senator.

While I've never had claims to stardom, my experience was only marginally different from Jimmy Stewart's character. But the venue wasn't the floor of the United States Senate: it happened at my first meeting of the Comox-Nanaimo Presbytery of the United Church, in the spring of 1993.

There, as in the Mr. Smith movie, it all came down to land, and who owns it.

I was welcomed that day as the newest and the youngest minister in the Presbytery, which takes in all of the United Churches on the northern half of Vancouver Island, where many of the early Indian missions, and two residential schools, were operated. My reception from the other ministers and delegates was very warm, deceptively so. And it was in this glow of what some clergy cynically call "the warm fuzzies" that I felt encouraged to get up during the debate on "native issues" and make what to me was a pretty innocuous proposal.

The topic that day was ministry to the Ahousaht Indians on the west coast, people of whom I knew virtually nothing. I had met a few Ahousahts in Port Alberni, but most of them live on Flores Island in

Love and Death in the Valley

the much-logged but majestic Clayoquot Sound, which is their ancestral homeland.

I also did not know that the Ahousahts had been the main victims of the local United Church residential school, and that Ahousaht land had been sold by that church for a profit to their financial backer MacMillan-Bloedel, the largest logging company in the province.

And so, not surprisingly, my words had a, shall we say, *disconcerting* impact on the church officials in attendance at the Presbytery meeting that day.

It was quite comical, actually. A very serious older minister named Oliver Howard had just given the "official" report on a century of church work with the Ahousahts which had spanned perhaps ten minutes. No mention of the residential schools, or anything controversial, crept its way into the grumpy guy's scant talk. But he did say how much the Ahousahts seemed to appreciate the coming of Christianity (and apparently, of smallpox and tuberculosis, I remember thinking); an appreciation that had been expressed to him by Ahousahts, it seemed, on many occasions.

In a burst of what amounted for him to evangelical fervour, the crusty minister concluded by exhorting us, "All this talk of land claims and sovereignty by the Indians doesn't mean anything if they aren't willing to come into the twentieth century and integrate into our culture. That's what we've been trying to show them all these years. So don't join in these attacks on our church missionaries and what they did. They were bringing the Good News to where it wasn't."

That didn't sit quite well, even with this throng of churchly yes-people. Oliver seemed to notice that, and so he quickly added,

"It isn't that the Indians here were savages, exactly. They were spiritually undeveloped. Their beliefs were just a preparation for the full revelation of God in Jesus Christ".

Nobody said anything at first. But it seemed like the right moment for me, so I stood up and said, "I'd like to suggest that we hold our next Presbytery meeting in Ahousaht, so we can hear from the people there themselves."

Boom! My words were like a bomb exploding among that complacent crowd. Three delegates actually jumped up and began shouting at the same time.

"They don't want us there!" blustered an old guy. "We've tried to be helpful, but they don't want anything to do with us!".

Another minister was saying something about the Ahousahts all being "dysfunctional people" when a woman near to me began hissing in my ear, "You just wait and see! In a few years they'll own the whole province!".

Wow! I thought, as more delegates shouted and spouted, and I wondered what the hell was going on. Talk about hitting a raw nerve!

My suggestion was never acted on, and delegates tended to avoid me for the rest of that day. But a church official named Bill Howie—who subsequently helped arrange my firing—gave me some "friendly advice" the next day. Again, I felt like I was part of a movie script, only this time from "The Godfather".

"You have a promising future with the church, Kevin, and a young family to provide for" Howie said with a flashy smile. "So be careful. Don't believe everything you hear about the native people here. Especially when it comes to Ahousahts."

Howie's veiled threat was not as important to me, at the time, as the general aversion of himself and his church colleagues to anything to do with the Ahousaht people. That intrigued me, and if anything made me more determined to get to know the Ahousahts. But I couldn't figure out what the big mystery was about these people, and their land; and why the church was so frightened of the whole subject.

Fortunately, at the same church meeting I first met Bruce Gunn, the minister to the Ahousahts and a kindred spirit. He smiled, and winked at me playfully over the Presbytery supper that night as he said, "Shit, you raised quite the tempest today. Want to know what it's all about?"

Seeing that I did, Bruce invited me up to the Ahousaht reserve later that week to help officiate at a funeral of one of their elders.

I had no idea of what to expect as I drove the snake-like road to the west coast, but it was enough to feel that the fog was parting a bit.

The Ahousahts live on Flores Island, which is a half-hour boat ride through the stormy, ocean-fed straits of the Clayoquot Sound. They lived there for thousands of years, fishing and whaling, and

Love and Death in the Valley

warring with local tribes like the Ohiats and the Ucluelets, until pale invaders came bearing crosses, and disease. By 1900, there were barely two hundred Ahousahts left alive out of the ten thousand who were there when the invaders arrived.

I remembered this as I stepped onto the dock at Marktosis, the main village, and I was greeted by Bruce Gunn and a frail native lady. I felt ashamed for who I was—a pale minister of a church that had murdered so many of her people—and I found it hard to look into her eyes. She didn't make my plight any easier when she said, "We don't like United Church ministers here too much. They never stay long; just long enough to steal something."

Bruce smiled when his friend said that, and he guided me through the clutter of sagging houses, dead cars, and screaming kids that was the village. We ended up in the church that he shared with the local Catholic priest.

"What did she mean by that?" I asked Bruce.

"You'll see" he said enigmatically as he shut the church door. In the back room sat an old Indian man sipping from a cup.

"This is Chief Earl Maquinna George" said Bruce. "You'll want to hear what he has to say."

The three of us sat there for the whole afternoon, while a sudden April squall pounded the windows and sent cold gusts through the walls and around our feet. Chief George did most of the talking.

By the end of that day, my view of the church had changed forever.

....

My world was shattering about me during that time, as I was receiving a rapid education about the "real" west coast, its hidden power structure, and its untold history. But it was still a private transformation. I didn't share what I was discovering with anyone, for it was too overwhelming. I wasn't sure whether I believed it all; I knew that I didn't want to believe it.

Did my church actually profit in stolen native land? Did it really infect native children with tuberculosis and let them die unattended, and then bury their bodies in secret? Was it a haven for pedophiles and murderers?

Chief Earl George believed so, as did every native person I spoke to. And later, after I had been expelled from the church, I discovered documents in government archives which confirmed the horror stories which so many native survivors had shared with me; like the report of the top Indian Affairs medical officer, Doctor Peter Bryce, who wrote in an official report in 1907,

"I believe the conditions are being deliberately created in our residential schools to spread infectious diseases ... The mortality rate in the schools often exceeds fifty percent. This is a national crime."

My daily duties as a minister gave me a rare access into the lives of not only aboriginal witnesses to these crimes, but native leaders, local politicians, and people on the ground who were living the effects of what amounted to planned genocide. And foremost in crimes of genocide, according to the United Nations, is the dislocation of a people off their land and into conditions of disease and death.

Chief Earl George was the first person to share with me the full details of the secret thefts of native land by the United Church that were arranged for the benefit of its business associates, like MacMillan-Bloedel. But the rot went far deeper.

It quickly became obvious that business, government and the church had been working together for more than a century to grab the lands and resources of west coast native people like the Ahousahts, using missionary work and the residential schools as a pretext to do so. It wasn't about "Christianising the heathen" at all, but about big money, and getting rid of the indigenous people, who prevented the European takeover by their continued occupation of the land.

"Anything was okay if it killed Indian people" Chief George told me that rainy day in Ahousaht, in the spring of 1993.

"They poisoned us, sterilised us, beat us to death in their schools, and killed the chiefs in secret if they didn't turn over their land. Everyone knows this, for these things all happened to us. It's only white people who can't believe it."

The chasm between the "two worlds" was becoming greater for me every day, and soon became unbreachable. I had to begin sharing

Love and Death in the Valley

what I knew with others in the church, for in my naivete I thought this would cause them to change, and face our past crimes.

I turned to native witnesses themselves to tell the story. My own role, as I saw it, was to create a protected space within which the "voiceless" could speak and be heard. And speak they did. One of the first of these was Alfred Keitlah.

Alfred was a small, elderly man who was a hereditary chief, and the official speaker for his clan. He and his son, Nelson, were the first native people to attend my church regularly. Alfred startled the pale congregants one Sunday morning in 1993 by standing up and breaking into prayer in his own language during our service.

The sound of Alfred's aged voice echoing in that bastion of "white" privilege, from where foreign missionaries had subjugated his people, gave me a chill of awe; others in church were less impressed. It was as if the ghosts of Alfred's people were reclaiming a sacred space stolen by Europeans. That, perhaps, was the moment when locked doors began to be opened in the Alberni Valley.

His son, Nelson, is one of the most powerful native politicians in the region, and a key player in treaty negotiations. He and I became good friends, and spent many hours at his home sharing stories and praying together.

When Alfred died that same year, his family drew even closer to me. After the funeral, I was introduced to the extended Keitlah clan, the younger members of whom were far more militant against the church and willing to talk about the residential schools, once they saw how sympathetic I was.

Unlike older Ahousahts and other natives, who tend to be devout and even fundamentalist Christians, most younger Indians lack any such allegiances towards Christianity. It was they who shared with me the first information about the hidden story of murder on the west coast.

I encouraged these younger people to come to my church and speak freely there, since I had an open pulpit policy and combined my sermon with comments and reflections from anyone in the congregation. By the second year of my ministry in Port Alberni, in the fall of 1993, this open door had swelled St. Andrew's from the twenty or so "white" parishioners it was when I arrived, to over one hundred worshippers on a Sunday, many of them younger, poorer, and aboriginal.

Those numbers stayed constant to the very day I was fired, a fact which shoots down the church hierarchy's later claim that I "divided and alienated" my Alberni congregation. Nothing is more untrue.

Every Wednesday, on food bank day, an army of hungry families descended on the church in a happy cacophony of screaming babies and kids who loved to race through the quiet sanctuary and poke around in the pews. I loved Wednesdays at St. Andrew's, as did many of our church members, even the old-timers. Many of them volunteered to bag and distribute groceries, and even drive families home to spare them the two mile walk from the "ghetto", as locals called it: the poor part of town where most of the off-reserve Indians live.

Some of them believed that simply by calling our food bank "Loaves and Fishes", miracles would be sure to happen there; and sure enough, they did.

Perhaps the most obvious one was how the racial barrier between "whites" and aboriginals that is so entrenched in Port Alberni began coming down every Wednesday. The reason became obvious to us soon. Not only were pale members of our church handing out food; they were also joining Indians in the food bank line in growing numbers because of the continual layoffs at MacMillan-Bloedel's pulp mill and logging camps.

A social ferment began brewing in the basement of our church: one that was directly challenging the local ruler, MacMillan-Bloedel, as well as the "white" establishment in town. The racist antagonism that, in any apartheid system, keeps poor people at each others' throats for the benefit of the wealthy, began to erode in the food bank line, and in our Sunday services. And the result was explosive.

By our second year together, we were doing more than hand out food. A dozen of us, both native and non-native activists in town, launched an anti-poverty group called Low Income Folks Together, or LIFT. This was the first community group in the history of the Alberni Valley that brought together Indians and "whites".

Even more threatening, LIFT wasn't just an advocacy group for the poor, but a political organization that raised questions about the reasons for such widespread poverty in the region. That inevitably pointed to MacMillan-Bloedel and its monopoly of the local land and the economy. By early 1994, LIFT had publicly raised a demand to the government to expropriate MacMillan-Bloedel's tree farm license and tax the corporation for all the jobs and income lost because of automation and layoffs.

We were challenging the local king for supremacy.

None of us knew, at the time, that MacMillan-Bloedel had a close financial relationship with the United Church, although the direct ties between prominent church officials like Fred Bishop and the company were obvious. Nor were we aware of the secret land deals between the company and the church at Ahousaht, Port Renfrew and on other west coast native territory, which also implicated the provincial government.

What we did know, quite intimately, was the fact that one out of three of us were below the poverty line, and couldn't feed our kids properly each month, while a dozen logging trucks roared out of the Valley every day, laden with old growth trees fetching millions of dollars.

The Indian members of LIFT knew that they were poor not just for economic reasons, but because of the refusal of local employers to hire natives, and the discriminatory housing practices that kept Indians ghettoized in the slum section of town. And every family suffered from the violence, the incest, and the addictions that were part of the legacy of the local Indian Residential School—a fact which was voiced more and more in LIFT meetings, and from my pulpit on Sundays.

These interlocking injustices became more apparent to our community, both in and outside of church. We were continually reminded of them by a group of native families who became church members and struggled against the odds to find a place among us.

They came from a group of slum apartments in "the ghetto", where mostly off-reserve Indians live. I had come to know them soon after I arrived in Port Alberni, when I delivered food to Karen Connerly and Charlie Sport, who lived with their three kids in the ghetto. Their eldest child, Charlie junior, had died of pneumonia the previous winter after the heat to their apartment went off, and the landlord refused to fix it for weeks on end.

Charlie and Karen began coming to church, and with them arrived others from their apartment block: mostly kids, a dozen or more of them, who were more than happy to be out of their slum, where they played each day among broken glass and abandoned cars.

The community that was being forged by these new arrivals was something to behold, from my perch at the front of the sanctuary: a sea of brown and pale faces, instead of the sad little group I had arrived to, now filled with all the noises and struggles of the community, and all its cries for help.

You just can't ignore a child. And so even the die-hard Old Guard in my congregation were forced to see the deeper reality of Port Alberni, and of the "white and native fact" in Canada, simply by coming to church every Sunday.

It's not normally like that in church. Worship time is a leap away from the daily and bitter facts of life, and death, for many of us. Our battered but hopeful souls come on Sundays to a place of refuge, where beautiful stories are told and things don't change, where God is guaranteed and love means being reconciled to people like yourself, not to total strangers.

And, of course, there are just so many seats in a church sanctuary.

All that changed in my congregation when the native children started filling the pews. Not even the hardest heart among us could turn away any of the hungry Indian kids. People had to shove over to fit them all in, making room not only for new bodies but other truths, and hidden histories.

The Indian children were the real, living witnesses to what our culture and our church had done to their people, and were still doing. Little six year old Eric Connerley, coughing from illnesses that never seemed to leave his frail body, and grabbing a handful of cookies in ravenous hunger, said more about aboriginal life on the west coast than did a hundred sermons. These children were the catalyst in what was transforming the hearts and minds of my congregants.

I noticed this in a very direct way whenever I performed a baptism of native children in church, and I'd walk with the little one in my arms around the entire sanctuary, introducing him, or her, to everyone there that day. I took a special delight in taking the baby up to one of the loggers who had been dragged to church by his wife, and waiting

Love and Death in the Valley

for an accepting grin to break over his formerly hard and cautious face.

The ice that had kept "whites" and natives in Port Alberni separate for generations began to break apart at such moments, and everyone in church knew it. A collective sigh of relief seemed to sweep through St. Andrew's then. But that kind of liberation does very funny and different things to people: it frees some, and terrifies others.

Anyone who came to my church was free to speak from the pulpit and vote at any meeting, and increasing numbers of people did so, on both sides of the colour line. That is how we first heard the stories of murders in the Alberni residential school, and of the deep racism in town that kept Indians jobless and stuck in slum housing.

Simply voicing these things was a clear-cut challenge to the local status quo. But a handful of newcomers to church did more than talk. They were five natives from the "ghetto", and they came to me one day after church for help.

I had come to know them at the food bank, and then in Bible study classes, but that day they gathered in my office to enlist my aid in confronting their landlord over their terrible housing.

I had baptised the sickly babies of these men and women over kitchen sinks, and I had buried some of their friends after they had taken their own lives, or been murdered. But now I was being asked to help them take on the local power structure in Port Alberni.

The landlord was a man named Gus Frigstad who lived in Nanaimo, and had a reputation for being the worst slum landlord in the area. There was rarely any running water or electricity in his apartments, and the buildings were in clear violation of local fire codes. The Port Alberni police chief even called them "death traps". And, as I began this story by relating, in the fall of 1995, one of our LIFT members, a native woman named Cecilia Joseph, burned to death in one of Frigstad's buildings because it lacked a door knob, fire alarms and extinguishers.

But Gus Frigstad had friends on city council, and in the local Anglican Church, and so he had never been prosecuted or even reprimanded for his breaking of the law, or for the one bedroom hovels where Indians shivered at the cost of $700 each month. Frigstad was part of the "white" establishment that has never had to answer for anything in the Alberni valley.

So the news that Frigstad was being taken to the Provincial Housing Arbitrator by some of his tenants struck the town, and our church, like the arrival of a rebel army: a sign of jubilation for those on the bottom, but definitely bad news for the group on top, like the chairman of my church board, former Port Alberni mayor and MacMillan-Bloedel executive, Fred Bishop.

Fred came to see me the day after *The Alberni Valley Times* had reported on the tenants' action against Frigstad. He asked me pointblank if I had been a part of it. I told him I had.

The look of betrayal in his eyes was unexpected. I had anticipated anger from him, but Fred treated me like a wayward son who needed moral correction.

"Gus Frigstad is a fine Christian man" he said to me sadly. "This will ruin his reputation in town."

"Why is he forcing kids to live in those dumps if he's a good Christian, Fred?" I responded.

Bishop shook his head disdainfully.

"Those people wreck wherever they live. They don't know how to provide for their children or stay off the bottle. I wouldn't be in Gus's shoes for all the money in the world."

Things went on in that vein until Bishop came to his main point.

"There are rules in any group, Kevin, and maybe you're forgetting where you are" he said slowly.

I told him I didn't understand.

"If you don't learn to be just a minister, Kevin, and stop all this social justice stuff, I won't be responsible ...".

His sudden silence said it all. I finally knew what was at stake.

That happened more than a year before I was summarily fired, and driven from the ministry, after I had exposed the church's secret dealings with MacMillan-Bloedel in stolen native land. And so it wasn't as if I had no warning of what was to come.

What surprised me, ultimately, was that it took the church and corporate power brokers that long to finally have me turfed from my pulpit. The fact that it did was because of the wide base of support that my ministry, and the work of LIFT, had within the community. This support protected me, for a little while.

Our efforts to improve housing in the ghetto paid off right away. Gus Frigstad was ordered by the government to renovate the buildings and conform to the provincial housing standards and fire codes. While this order was lauded as a victory for tenants by local community activists, and won LIFT new support and prestige in the valley, it boomeranged back on the tenants themselves. For Frigstad used the renovations as a justification to raise all of their rents, and most of our people were forced to move, into equally slumy apartments in the ghetto.

A backlash happened against them, as well, at my church. LIFT members were denied the use of the building for their meetings, and were shunned on Sundays. And, as the chairman of the church board, Fred Bishop began pressuring the congregation to close our Loaves and Fishes food bank, which was, to him and his friends, the source of all the "trouble".

And so, the simple and nominally "Christian" act of opening my church to the poor and the strangers among us began triggering events that would explode by my third year at St. Andrew's, and reveal hidden crimes. But none of this was expected by any of us; especially not by me. At the time, I was just trying to be a good minister, which for me meant "leaving the ninety-nine to find the one lost sheep".

Doing so in Port Alberni, of course, is a tumultuous thing to do, for the church and the entire culture there rests on the bones of thousands of murdered people, and on the suffering of their descendents, who were by and large the ones speaking from my pulpit about their oppression, and demanding a change.

It's often said that a new minister's first year with his congregation is like a honeymoon; everything seems to turn out for the best, and people are on their good behaviour. By the second and third years, reality sets in, and positioning for power begins among all the different cliques in the church. So it was at St. Andrew's.

By the fall of 1994, my third year had begun, and the congregation had tripled in size, and become poorer, younger, and more aboriginal, although three older white families still ruled the roost. These families—the Spencers, the Barkers, and the Grays, along with Fred Bishop—felt directly threatened by the "invasion" (as one of them called it) of all those "others" on Sunday morning, and they told me so.

I didn't know at the time how directly these families were linked not only to the local establishment—namely, MacMillan-Bloedel—

but to the Alberni residential school officials who were later charged with murdering native children. But I discovered so quickly, as they began to react more hostilely to the new aboriginal voices in church, and to their calls for justice. Small wonder, since these "white" families had relatives, living and dead, who would be implicated if the truth about the residential school ever came out. Fred Bishop and his group had much to lose by the words of native people resounding in the walls of St. Andrew's.

Of course, others besides the Old Guard were threatened by the survivors' voices. Very powerful interests came to bear to shut down our new ministry at St. Andrew's, and my career in the church, beginning with MacMillan-Bloedel and its friends in government and the United Church hierarchy. For that ministry was doing what is always unacceptable to the powerful, and the guilty: opening a window on crimes of both the past and the present, and empowering those with the details of those crimes to act.

Many forces were converging on our little chapel in the north end of a dying mill town by the fall of 1994, as if that time and place had become the focal point in a greater battle. The lines were clearly drawn by then, between the rump of settler families around Fred Bishop who were determined to keep the church, and the town, exactly the same, and the larger but uncoordinated group of native and poor families who saw our church as a way to change the community in their interest.

Like two belligerent armies, these groups examined the other every Sunday, weighing their options, and wondering who would fire the first shot—and how the resulting battle would end.

Being more experienced, and more ruthless, the Old Guard struck first, and aimed its blow expertly at the head of its enemy—a blow designed to decapitate our movement, confuse it, and send the "others" in church packing.

I was the public symbol of the new changes in church, and in Port Alberni; my work as the town's "crusading minister" was regularly reported in the local newspaper. But another half-dozen people were also the core of our movement's leadership. Within a few months of my sudden firing in January, 1995, all of these people had been driven from the church, lost their jobs, and become marginalized in town, and two of them died by so-called "suicide" the next year.

Love and Death in the Valley

The big boot came down on our fledgling revolution before we even knew it.

By the time this happened, our church had become a literal lifeboat for many people in Port Alberni, both materially and spiritually. That boat was torpedoed by the events that ended my life as a United Church minister.

Besides closing the church to "outsiders" after I was fired, the Old Guard ended all the social programs and food distributions that so many people required. Our food bank was shut down without warning one week after my firing, in the middle of winter, when over two hundred families depended on it for life itself.

The United Church claimed, at the time, that it couldn't "afford" the $1200 a month that it was spending to keep our Loaves and Fishes food bank running. But somewhere in its coffers, the same church found over $250,000 to spend on having me expelled from its ministerial ranks, the following year!

Something was serious enough, at least in the minds of the power brokers of the United Church, to fire me without cause, drive me from the ministry, and concoct an elaborate kangaroo court procedure to "de-frock" and discredit me, regardless of the cost involved.

A significant clue to what that "something" was occurred just before I was fired, on October 17, 1994: a turning point for me that will mark my life until I die. For on that date, I wrote a letter to the church officialdom objecting to its secret and illegal sale of Ahousaht land, Lot 363, to MacMillan-Bloedel. It was a letter that sealed my fate in the church, ending my work, my career, and even my family.

I had known about the Lot 363 deal since Chief Earl George had told me about it the previous year, during my first visit to Ahousaht. Earl himself had been stone-walled by the United Church when he tried to get the land returned to his people. Even more ominously, church officials had frozen all funding for Earl's training for ministry after he raised the Lot 363 scandal. The church was clearly coming down hard on Earl for spotlighting their secret business agreements. And yet, frankly, I didn't know then whether I should stick out my neck—and that of my family, and the ones who depended on my ministry—over this one issue of stolen native land.

An incident in October of 1994 prompted me to do so, at the regular meeting of my Presbytery, where church officials lied and distorted the facts about Lot 363, and slandered Chief George and other Ahousaht elders. Sadly, my objection to these lies—which I discuss in the next chapter—gave the Old Guard at St. Andrew's, and their friends in the church hierarchy, the justification they felt they needed to move against my ministry, and destroy the flowering movement that was giving life and hope to those who had neither.

Somewhere in me I felt a showdown was coming. I instinctively responded by gathering together the core leaders of LIFT, all of whom were coming to church each Sunday, and praying together one night in the sanctuary. I remember asking God for courage, and to not let me abandon those who needed me the most.

The others knew what was coming, too, for having been poor and under the boot their whole lives, they were total realists. So instead of our usual heated rounds of debate and planning, we just held hands and prayed, going deep, waiting, and hoping.

We parted in silence, except for Krista Lynn. She was a small Metis woman who didn't survive what was about to crash down on all of us; she was found dead, possibly murdered, in her slum apartment the following year after she had spoken out against the abduction of native children into the pedophile ring in town. But that night, she was more alive and clear than any of us, especially me.

Krista touched my arm and almost whispered, "You don't have to be afraid, Kev. It's all going to be for God's purpose, whatever happens. I know you feel a lot like our Lord did in Gethsemane. You're going to go to your Cross alone. You're going to have a lot of lonely nights ahead. You're going to feel completely alone. But the Lord will be there alongside you, 'cause you'll be doing his will."

The words of this impoverished woman have been one of the lifelines I have held on to over the cruel years since that October night in 1994. I was not there for Krista when she died, but her vision was there for me at that crossroads moment when my faith could have left me, and all would have been lost.

It was my final comfort before darkness filled the land.

Love and Death in the Valley

```
                                    R.R.3, Site 304, C-30,
                                    Port Alberni,
                                    B.C.   V9Y 7L7.

                                    27th. January, 1995
```

To Whom It May Concern

I would like you to know how I feel about Reverend Kevin McNamee-Annett.

Kevin is a person with the utmost integrity and honesty. I came from the Catholic Church to the United Church solely due to Kevin. His caring attitude is outstanding and he is simply the best minister I have come across. I do not say this lightly as I have always attended Church and am now fifty years oldso. I have had the experience of many different priests and ministers.

Kevin has put himself out to help the poor of this community and has never counted the cost to himself or spared his time. He to me embodies true christianity by being involved and active. He does not court the rich and powerful but rather spends his energies on helping the disadvantaged. His sermons are the most uplifting, educational and thought-provoking I have ever heard and are proof of a lot of time spent.

I am sorry that he will no longer be here where he is sorely needed, for he is the best and brightest of ministers.

Penelope O'Connell

Penelope O'Connell

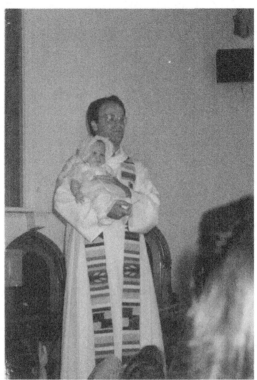

'Rev Kev' and his daughter at her baptism, St. Andrew's United Church, Port Alberni, September 1992

The Eternal Vigil: Harriett Nahanee, Alberni Residential School survivor and witness to the murder of Maisie Shaw by Reverend Alfred Caldwell, July 1996

Love and Death in the Valley

Ahousaht children on the dock of Marktosis village,
Flores Island, May 1995

Kevin Annett

Former minister alleges officials killed students

Native kids 'used for' experiments

THE VANCOUVER SUN, WEDNESDAY, APRIL 26, 2000

'Babies buried under apple tree'

"I found a 16-year-old native girl beaten to death, with no clothes on,"
— HARRY WILSON

Maisie Shaw died in 1946 after being kicked down a flight of stairs by an employee.
— Dr. Dennis Tallio – Penelakut

school's grim litany of death

Stories by Suzanne Fournier
Staff Reporter

Beverley and Carolyn recovered.

A14 THE VANCOUVER SUN, SATURDAY, APRIL 10, 1999

A long table held the names of hundreds of children who died at Kuper Island school — from disease, from accidents and from suspicious causes.

Penelakut organizer Diane Harris told her same story: "Babies were buried under that apple tree, born to girls who had been sexually abused by priests."

"We've asked the area, but they not just sexual a death we want po The Kuper Isla from 1890 to 197 and Oblate Cathol Oblate Brother convicted of sex boys in the '60s, other sexual-ab

Police told of death at residential school

PORT ALBERNI

NATION

— Colonist, September 24, '9

UN panel condemns Canada's treatment of aboriginal

34

In The Ghetto: Slum Housing in Port Alberni, 1993

Kevin Annett

Vancouver Sun, July 10, 1995

AT LARGE

Minister who tried to bring natives into the fold fired by his church

PORT ALBERNI

Nu-Chah-Nulth peoples have associated with the United Church since it dispatched fervent missionaries to snag souls in remote settlements a hundred years ago.

Yet Rev. Kevin McNamee-Annett, newly arrived in Port Alberni from an activist street ministry in Toronto, observed that almost no natives attended his new church.

"They never set foot in our church. I found that strange."

George Hamilton, a young native, retired from Vancouver's tough East Side streets to make his kids. He says he felt the lack of Port Alberni's aboriginal prejudice while he was growing up.

"As a kid, I don't remember one Indian face working in any of the stores in town. I still don't see any Indian faces working in any of the stores. But Kevin, Kevin didn't just have compassion for Indians. He had compassion for all the poor and weak."

Hamilton became one of McNamee-Annett's parishioners. McNamee-Annett says he did set out to change things. He counselled abuse victims at the native friendship centre. He ran workshops. He started a food bank. Many of its users were native and he says he became close to them.

"In the poor part of the town and on the reserve some of the housing is the worst I've ever seen — and I've done urban ministries in Toronto, Vancouver and Winnipeg," Annett says. "The traditional congregation was fairly uptight."

McNamee-Annett says some families he encouraged to begin attending church services ran into a chilly climate. When he suggested at one board meeting that the neglected, burying the dispossessed. His ministry took him into the wretched strip that natives call The Ghetto. It still seems invisible to Port Alberni's comfortable middle class.

"When nobody else spoke out," says Hamilton, "there was Kevin."

McNamee-Annett says he simply sought to ground lost souls in his church, welcoming them. Sunday attendance doubled. He told his flock to "learn to love them, up close. For love of the stranger is the only measure by which you and I will be judged."

Some of the congregation didn't like it. Loving strangers was okay in theory, it seems, but not in practice.

"To bring the natives into the pews was explosive," McNamee-Annett says.

He chose the young mother. One of his parishioners quit. On Jan. 8,

STEPHEN HUME

board meeting that the neglected Nelson Keitlah serve on a church committee the silence was "deafening."

One day a young woman from the poorest part of Port Alberni brought her little son to church. The baby cried, as babies do. This bothered him. But for some members of the congregation, it was a final, infuriating straw.

"Two women went to her and told her to get out. They said her baby was a little brat. 'Why did you bring him here, we don't want you.' They later came to me and threatened to leave if she stayed."

It was, he says, a dilemma to test his faith.

"It was 'suffer the little children to come unto me' versus good religions with the congregation."

he notified the church of his intention to resign effective June 30. Two weeks later, he says, he was summarily fired at the behest of six parishioners.

"The only reason church officials have given for this sudden, harsh action is that certain unidentified members of St. Andrew's had criticisms of my sermons and ministry. I have letters supporting the minister," wrote a strong letter supporting the minister. At one point, the Ahousat bothered her objection to the church's sale, for substantial profit, of a property it had been more or less given by the native community for a school.

That, Keitlah believes, was the real source of his lack of support from the church hierarchy.

Church authorities decline to comment on the reasons for the firing. Authorities do confirm that it was not a disciplinary matter and that it had nothing to do with moral misconduct. They claim it was not connected to his ministry to poor natives.

"It's important to remember that there are good people here," says Keitlah. "People were kind to me. But he admits he has stopped attending the church since McNamee-Annett was dismissed.

"My faith in God isn't shaken," Hamilton says, "but it is certainly shaken in the church. It was, 'Get them out of here! We don't want them here!' It was gross.

"I wouldn't paint the entire congregation with the same brush — there is a silent majority. It's an indictment of them that they were silent. I have no desire to attend that church."

"I think it's just atrocious what they did to him," says Jack McDougall of Port Alberni's Métis Association. "His actions spoke louder than words — so do theirs."

As for the jobless reverend? McNamee-Annett says he will be preaching the gospel. Church or no church:

"They've taken away my job but not my calling." □

The First Account of Kevin Annett's story, in The Vancouver Sun, 10 July, 1995

Chapter Two: Land-Grabs and Empty Stomachs, or A Tale of Two Letters

"Stamp and Sproat purchased the land for about twenty pounds in goods, but the land transaction with the Indians troubled Sproat ... Since the Indians did not recognise the colonial authority in Victoria and had sold the land only under the threat of a loaded cannon pointed at them, it was obvious to Sproat the land had been taken by force."

Description of the first European seizure of land in the Alberni Valley in 1860 by Government Agent Gilbert Sproat, in **The Albernis** by Jan Peterson (1992)

I think it's obvious that the church's national office removed you because they knew of the upcoming RCMP investigation into the residential schools and the Ahousaht land deal. They were in for a rough fight and didn't want dissent from a Port Alberni pulpit.

Rev. Bruce Gunn in a letter to the author, March 3, 1999

Those church men insulted me and my people. They treated me like I was a child and I didn't matter. They never change.

Chief Earl Maquinna George of the Ahousaht Nation to the author, February 12, 1995

The lies that I had heard at the Presbytery meeting of mid October, 1994 so troubled me that I wrote a letter about it to the church officials who had uttered them. I was tossed out of my pulpit by those same men less than two months later.

Everyone on the west coast, pale or native, knows that things often boil down to a simple question: *Who owns the land?* My people, and my church, had invaded and destroyed the west coast Indian nations precisely to grab their land. The lies that I took issue with in October of 1994, and was fired and "excommunicated" for confronting, involved the ownership of ancestral land of the Ahousaht Nation on Flores Island, otherwise known as "Lot 363".

My church claimed that it had "bought" this ancestral territory from the Ahousahts in 1904, and therefore had every right to sell it for a profit to the grandson of its first missionary to the Ahousahts, a businessman named Hamilton Ross who was connected to MacMillan-Bloedel. The Ahousaht elders said the opposite: the land was not for sale, and so the church never owned it, and had engaged in theft when it sold what wasn't theirs to a close friend of the church.

The Ahousahts wanted their land back. But now it was in the grasping paws of MacMillan-Bloedel, which gave the local United Church an appreciative $8000 donation that same year. So the church, not surprisingly, said no to the Ahousahts, and lied to their members by telling them that the Ahousahts were making the whole thing up.

There were no Ahousahts at the fateful meeting of Comox-Nanaimo Presbytery when the Lot 363 arrangement was presented to me, and a hundred other delegates, in a church hall in Gold River on the weekend of October 16 and 17, 1994. There were no aboriginal people there at all, in fact. That wouldn't have fit the colonial pattern.

Instead, the Ahousahts were misrepresented by pale men who saw the land as their own, and the issue as being one of keeping secret arrangements in place: like the one between their church and MacMillan-Bloedel, which needed Lot 363 and its precious preserve of old-growth cedar trees. And the overwhelming message given to we Presbytery delegates that weekend was not to rock that lucrative boat.

I wasn't prepared to, at first. The whole matter of Lot 363 seemed distant and irrelevant to what I was building at my own church. But when Presbytery officials began telling bald-faced lies to the delegates about Chief Earl George and other Ahousaht elders, I could not sit there and be party to such a massive deceit.

For one thing, senior church officers were claiming that Chief George had refused to meet with them or the provincial government to discuss Lot 363, when I knew from conversations with him that the Chief had tried on many occasions to sit down with both parties in order to get his peoples' land back, and he had been rebuffed. The Presbytery had even <u>refused</u> to allow any Ahousahts to sit on the church committee dealing with Lot 363, the previous year. It was the

United Church and the government who were turning a deaf ear to the Ahousahts, and not surprisingly, since both church and state were financially tied to MacMillan-Bloedel as major shareholders and recipients of company donations.

The Presbytery officers were calling Chief George a liar in public, and with a thinly-veiled racism, in order to cover their own theft of and profiteering in native land, and their links with MacMillan-Bloedel.

"We've come to expect this kind of thing from the Ahousahts" declared Oliver Howard, the former west coast missionary and my immediate predecessor at St. Andrew's who I referred to earlier. "They aren't reliable when it comes to showing up for meetings or keeping their committments. We've tried our best to show them that Lot 363 was church property, but they're completely unreasonable. All they have to prove their claim to the land are their own primitive oral records, which aren't any more reliable than their memory."

With a smug smile, Howard concluded to the Presbytery delegates, "So the next time you hear them going on about their treaty rights and claims to the whole province, remember who you're dealing with: people who... well, let's just say, people who like to stretch the truth."

In other words, "White Man Knows Best, since White Man is Best". When has that refrain ever changed? I wondered as Howard spoke.

To see such white supremacy so "alive and well" in the heart of the officially "progressive" United Church of Canada was more than shocking to me. It made me see that little had changed in a century, and I was part of a church that was still waging war on aboriginal people in order to get their land for corporate benefactors.

If not exactly like Paul on the Damascus road, I was at least beginning to have my old allegiances shaken.

Every week, I was preaching to my congregation that our principles meant nothing unless they were practiced daily, and up-close. How, then, could I look the other way when my church's leaders were engaging in such racism and deceit for the sake of money and power?

All of this was turning over in my mind as I drove home to Port Alberni that same night. By the time I pulled into our driveway, I was already composing a letter to the Presbytery Executive about the events of that day, and Lot 363.

You can read the letter I wrote below. It asked the Presbytery officials to arrange the return of Lot 363 to the Ahousahts, as our own church policy compelled them to do. I mailed it off to the Executive the next morning, and I never heard back from them. But within a week of their receiving it, two of their members—former classmates of mine and fellow ministers, Phil Spencer and Foster Freed—began holding secret meetings with Fred Bishop and others on my church's official board to arrange my removal from St. Andrew's.

Perhaps what worried the Presbytery officials about my letter was my statement that I would not publicly associate myself with the church on the Lot 363 issue unless they, the Presbytery leaders, conformed to United Church policy on native land claims, and sought to return all of Lot 363 to the Ahousaht people. I can't say. All I know is that my fate was sealed after I wrote the letter; a fact admitted by the church hierarchy at my formal "delisting" trial that expelled me from the ministry two years later. For Win Stokes, a senior Presbytery officer from Gold River, said on record at that trial,

We had no concerns about Kevin at all until he wrote his letter about Lot 363, in October of 1994. Then something had to be done ... A senior government official told me at that time, 'We can't have Kevin upset the applecart over Lot 363; there's too much at stake.'"
(October 9, 1996)

Ironically, at this very moment, when a few church, and probably corporate and government, officials were arranging my firing without any authorization or due process, my own congregation was reaffirming my work and position at St. Andrew's. At a special retreat held that same month at Moorecroft camp, over sixty of our church members voted unanimously to approve my ministry and "enthusiastically" recommend to the official board that my call be extended.

A palace coup is always covert, however, and only three of my church board members knew at that time about the secret manuverings by the Presbytery Executive to have me removed. These same three people—Fred Bishop, Anne Gray and Wendy Barker—

were the core of the church's "Old Guard", and they quickly struck against me.

It came right out of the blue, as assassinations always do.

In early December, I was asked by Fred Bishop to attend a "special meeting" of my personnel committee, at Anne Gray's home. When I arrived, only three members of the committee, Bishop, Gray, and Wendy Barker, were present, and they all sat stone-faced around a table. The committee's fourth member, Sharon Simpson, who was a well-known friend of mine and a supporter of my work, was unexplainably absent.

Fred did most of the talking. He was the ex-Mayor of the town, after all, and used to this kind of hatchet-job thing.

He told me that "many people" in the congregation were "dissatisfied" with my ministry, and that unless I did three things I would have to either resign or be fired. Those things were: immediately close our Loaves and Fishes food bank, stop visiting "non-members", and stop preaching about social justice issues.

I was too shocked to say anything, at first. Part of me wasn't surprised at his words, because I knew how much Bishop personally detested the food bank and all those "non-members"—his own euphemism for Indians—coming to church. But I hadn't expected so blatant and unsophisticated an attack.

He, and the others, were very nervous, and seemingly under pressure to get me out, as quickly as they could. Like the other church mandarins who would later "delist" me, Bishop and his cronies were compelled by this pressure into coarse methods and bald-faced lies.

His unsupported claim of widespread "dissatisfaction" in the congregation, for instance.

"If there's so many people upset with me, then why didn't any of them speak about it at our congregational retreat?" I asked Bishop. "Why would I have received a unanimous vote of approval just weeks ago, if what you say is true?".

Such simple logic seemed to confuse Bishop for a moment, but the old politician rebounded with the same ultimatum.

"You have until next week to give us your decision. Otherwise, we'll have to ask for your immediate resignation."

The other two said very little. Anne Gray glared at me loathingly, while Wendy Barker scribbled notes the entire time, which Bishop described as the "minutes" of our conversation. Those minutes of what Bishop assured me was a wholly "confidential" meeting were in the hands of top church officials by the next day, and, <u>in complete violation of church rules</u>, the "confidential" minutes were shared generally with members of the Presbytery Executive. I have never been allowed to see a copy of those minutes, after many requests for one.

I remember telling Bishop and the others, half in shock, that they didn't represent the whole congregation, but only a faction in it, and that I would appeal their action to the entire board. None of them said a thing; not even a word of regret. Numbed, I drove home.

After I was summarily fired the next month, the United Church hierarchy had to scramble to produce a reason for my removal, since they never gave me one; indeed, they continually stated that there were no charges against me. They kept changing the reason for firing me, however, depending on the need of the moment, but an early version they hit on was that I "failed to recognise the authority of Presbytery", which implied that I was antagonistic towards that body and wouldn't work with it.

Nothing is more untrue. In fact, the first thing I did after receiving the ultimatum from Fred Bishop and his flunkies was to go to the Presbytery Executive and ask for their assistance. In my naivete, I didn't realise that Bishop was acting at the behest of the same Presbytery Executive, which by then had resolved to remove me from my pulpit because of my Lot 363 letter. Nevertheless, I asked the Executive to fulfil its mandate as a "collegial and conciliatory body of support for clergy", and intervene at St. Andrew's to stop one faction from having me thrown out of my church.

In response to my request, three new figures from the Executive stepped in: Bob Stiven, Colin Forbes, and Cameron Reid, all top Presbytery officials who were instrumental in the decision to remove me after I wrote my letter objecting to the sale of Lot 363 in Ahousaht. But instead of being neutral peace-makers, they openly took sides with Fred Bishop and supported his ultimatum to me, despite the fact that it was a demand of only three people that was never voted on or endorsed by my church board, or anyone else, for that matter.

Clearly, the writing was on the wall. Presbytery was my formal employer, and its officials were reneging on their contractual obligations to me by siding with a few congregants in an openly partisan move to oust me, against the stated wishes of the majority of church members. And so the outcome was never in doubt. I had very little time left at St. Andrew's, or in the United Church of Canada.

Neither did Chief Earl George. For at precisely this same time, during the Christmas holidays of 1994, he was forced from the church by the same men who were arranging my ouster, and for the same reason: he had written a letter to the Presbytery objecting to the sale of Lot 363 in Ahousaht.

Earl's letter had been sent earlier than mine, and to more people, but the result was the same, for MacMillan-Bloedel's final acquisition of the Ahousaht land was due to be completed by the new year of 1995. **This was the date established by the "Interim Measures Agreement" between the provincial government and local native tribes, by when treaty issues were to be resolved; and, unless MacMillan-Bloedel had obtained the land by this time, the whole deal might have collapsed.**

Suddenly, then, the two public critics of the Lot 363 deal—Chief George and myself—became a tremendous liability to not only the company, but the United Church, the government, and those native leaders who stood to profit by the arrangement. And so Earl and I were quickly forced from the church, maligned, and marginalized at precisely the same time.

Earl's letter had been more potentially damaging to these conspirators, for as the Keeper of the Land for his people, he had an obligation under tribal law to protect their ancestral territory from all logging. As such, he claimed all of Lot 363 in his letter, which was sent to the United Church and the provincial government. And as a result, the Provincial Forester, Paul Pashnik, halted all logging on that land and ordered everyone involved, including the United Church, to work things out.

The church never forgave Chief George for thrusting them back into the Lot 363 spotlight, since the supposedly "progressive" United Church was suddenly exposed as a profiteer in stolen native land. MacMillan-Bloedel ended up getting all of the land anyway, and the church was spared any negative publicity by their man in government, Reverend John Cashore, who, as Aboriginal Affairs minister at the time, manoeuvred the church out of negotiations and played a behind-the-scenes role in disposing of Chief George and myself. But, with the same vindictive purpose they showed towards me, church officials retaliated against Chief George.

Prior to writing his letter, the aging Ahousaht Chief had been enthusiastically accepted by the United Church as the first west coast native elder to apply for ordination as one of its ministers. But in 1993, after the Lot 363 scandal exploded, Chief George's funding for theological training suddenly disappeared, and he was denied any assistance from the church, without explanation. The church refused to even respond to Earl's frantic inquiries.

Finally, during the same week before Christmas of 1994 that I was being forced from my pulpit, the same three Presbytery officials who set up my expulsion, Bob Stiven, Colin Forbes and Cameron Reid, met with Chief George and told him that he was no longer a candidate for ministry in the United Church.

I visited Chief George shortly after that, and he was dejected but angry.

"Those church men insulted me and my people" he said, describing the humiliation of being thrown out of the ordination process without any reason. "They treated me like I was a child and I didn't matter. They never change."

Earl's rapid expulsion was like a warning sign for me, but by then it was too late. The same hangmen were closing in on me.

Little did I know at that time, but the national office of the United Church, and its Moderator Marion Best, had already been alerted to my objection to the sale of Lot 363. Within a week of my writing the letter to Presbytery, Best had been given a copy of it, and assigned John Siebert, a church official, to "deal" with the matter, along with Brian Thorpe, the B.C. Conference official who soon after arranged my dismissal and delisting. Thorpe and Siebert bribed Ahousaht chiefs with $14,000 to distance themselves from both Chief Earl George and myself.

The Ahousaht minister, Bruce Gunn, confirmed this conspiracy in a letter to me in March of 1999. Bruce wrote,

> "I'm convinced your removal was orchestrated from Toronto, from the church head office. Just a week after you wrote your letter about the Ahousaht land deal, Marion Best had a copy of that letter ... That would have been on the first weekend of November, 1994. Within a month of that, John Siebert of the head office was onto the case.
>
> "I think it's obvious that the national office removed you because they knew of the upcoming RCMP investigation, and of the land deal, after Marion Best got your letter. They were in for a rough fight and didn't want dissent from a Port Alberni pulpit ... There's no question that John Cashore, as Aboriginal Affairs minister, tried to run interference for the church, and sidetrack the church connection to the land deal using government money, as early as the spring of 1994.
>
> "The payoff to the Ahousaht band council came from the United Church after a conference call with John Siebert and Brian Thorpe that arranged to pay ... $7000 to the band council by way of the church's nothern native group, run by Jim Angus. This $7000 went directly to the Ahousaht band council, and another $7000 bill for research was picked up by the church, making it a $14,000 payoff in all.
>
> "The church was at this time cutting off Earl George's funding for ministerial training, and spreading rumours and smears against Earl among the Ahousahts. This whole thing was orchestrated mostly by Brian Thorpe with help from John Siebert." *(affidavit of March 3, 1999)*

Farcically, the same John Siebert attempted to pass himself off as an "independent researcher into residential schools", in early 2001, and received much press coverage across Canada with his criminal claim that the damages to native children in residential schools were "minimal", and caused by "many other factors" other than the schools!

With typical superficiality, the media did not bother to mention the fact that, hardly the "unbiased" researcher they presented him as, Siebert is a major "spin doctor" for the church who played a direct role in covering-up the Lot 363 scandal and driving both Chief George and myself out of the United Church.

As this campaign to crush us approached, I struggled to shield my wife of the time, Anne McNamee, from what was coming, for she suffered from chronic depression and lacked the fortitude to cope with my railroading out of the church, and the other brutalities being heaped on us. The church officials knew this, and, according to Anne's lawyer, approached her over the next month and enlisted her aid in their campaign against me, including providing them with information about my plans.

The church eventually rewarded Anne for her role as informant when it intervened aggressively in our subsequent divorce the next year, and helped her win custody of our two children in a Vancouver court.

First, Presbytery official Phil Spencer gave her lawyer confidential and libelous documents that she used against me in her divorce and custody action. Brian Thorpe then suddenly released a statement to the press during the very week our custody issue was before the courts which stated, falsely, that the church was insisting that I undergo a "psychiatric examination".

This inexplicable and unethical action by Thorpe resulted in an article by Thorpe's close personal friend, Vancouver Sun reporter Doug Todd, entitled *"Fired Minister Ordered to Undergo Psychiatric Exam."* Two days after this article was published, Anne was awarded sole custody of our two young daughters by the court.

Unable to even imagine such deceit and betrayal at that time, my main concern over Christmas of 1994 was whether or not I should resign, or wait to be fired, which was inevitable after the Presbytery officials openly allied with Fred Bishop and his faction. Anne and I decided that I should resign, since if I was to apply for another church posting elsewhere, I needed to do so before very long into the new year.

Since providing for my family was paramount, I resigned from St. Andrew's in a letter to my church board on January 8, 1995, asking that I be allowed to work until June 30. My resignation was accepted "with very great regret", and my request to work to the end of June was granted.

These facts are important, since in the wake of their gutting of me and their own rule book, and of my role in exposing the Lot 363 land deal and residential school crimes, United Church leaders have concocted a fabricated version of my fate, and my ministry, which is designed to discredit me and what I have uncovered. The church's version bears no resemblance to reality.

Distorting the facts about my case has been the norm for church officials, of course, from the beginning of these sick cruelties. Long before I was removed from my pulpit, Presbytery officers were telling members of my congregation that I was "mentally unstable", and was facing dismissal, according to Gerry Walerius, a long-standing board member at St. Andrew's.

In fact, Walerius relates that a secret meeting was held with the entire church board shortly before my dismissal, at which Presbytery officers Bob Stiven and Cameron Reid stated *"that the decisions made by St. Andrew's board were not going to be followed. They stated that Kevin was about to be removed as minister immediately ... The Board was told not to divulge any of this information to Kevin."* (See below)

I knew nothing of this, at the time. But, a few days after this secret board meeting, Gerry Walerius alluded to me that I was facing dismissal. I immediately phoned Bob Stiven and asked him to meet me at my office so that I could confirm this rumour about my fate.

He met me on January 20, and brought along Colin Forbes, another Presbytery official. I asked them point-blank whether I was about to be fired.

"Absolutely not" said Stiven quickly, his narrow eyes darting about my office.

Suspecting the worst, I asked him again, "Are you telling me that I am not facing any kind of disciplinary action or dismissal?"

Stiven nodded his head, and Colin Forbes interjected, with a smile, "You have nothing to worry about."

Both men were openly lying to me, since my dismissal was in the works as they spoke to me; a fact they had already shared with my board members. But, foolishly, I took them at their word. And so I was genuinely surprised when the axe fell on me three days later.

But before then was my final service as minister of St. Andrew's, on January 22: my eldest daughter Clare's sixth birthday. The Old Testament reading that day was the story of Abraham's near-execution of his son Isaac after God told the patriarch to kill his own flesh and blood. I knew in my guts that my own ritual killing was approaching, and so in my sermon I spoke about how practising mercy was more important than doing what some higher power told you to do.

My congregants must have known what I was referring to, since most of them knew about my impending dismissal, even when I didn't. Many of them were openly crying during the service, including even some of the Old Guard. Fred Bishop wouldn't look at me the whole hour. The church felt like a funeral was happening, and after the service, many people took my hand, hugged me in silence, or gave me long, sad looks. They were being forced to comply with not only my secret removal, but the killing of a bold and beautiful opening up of their church, and they hated themselves for it. But still they remained mute.

The handful of executioners waited until the next day to strike, so that I couldn't speak about my firing from my pulpit.

The next morning, Monday, January 23, 1995, I was feeding my youngest daughter Elinor and was preoccupied, as always, with other peoples' problems. A family of five had just disembarked in town without any money, and had come to me for help. I was trying to figure out how to feed and house all of them when the telephone rang. It was one of the top officials of the United Church in British Columbia, a weasly little man named Art Anderson.

In the sixteenth century, church Inquisitors wore crosses and used iron and fire to "cleanse" their victims, or so went their cold logic. Today, they look like businessmen and use as their weapons rules which they themselves never follow. But, then or now, the Inquisitor believes that error must be rooted out; and the error always exists in the intended victim, and never in the church, or the Inquisitor.

I'd be insulting such renowned butchers as Torquemada or Thomas Aquinas if I compared their sophisticated means of uprooting "heresy" to the dull expediency of United Church Inquisitors like Art Anderson, so I won't stretch the analogy too far. And yet Anderson's actions were as lethal as any of his antecedents.

Love and Death in the Valley

Art Anderson is retired now, to wherever it is that moral midgets end up. But in January of 1995, he was, unfortunately, the personnel officer of the United Church in British Columbia; "the equivalent of a Bishop" he liked to boast, inaccurately, to those ministers he chose to crush.

In such a role, Anderson was the hatchet-man who summarily fired me without any notice or cause. He wasn't allowed to do so, even according to the United Church Manual. But of course that didn't stop him, for his power was absolute, and unaccountable.

When he phoned me at my home that morning he was already at St. Andrew's. He and Cameron Reid of the Presbytery wanted to see me right away.

His sudden appearance in town seemed odd, but I didn't expect that anything was up. I had already offered my resignation to the church. The Old Guard were acting openly relieved now that "their" church was back in their hands. I was losing my congregation, and the community that I had built with such sacrifice, and I was leaving many friends in the Alberni valley; so I couldn't imagine that the church officialdom would want more blood from me.

And yet the Beast, it seems, is insatiable.

So, more curious than anything, I met Anderson at the church, along with my wife Anne. Anderson was already sitting in my office with Cameron Reid, who looked like a sad little gnome.

Expressionless, Anderson handed me a letter which immediately dismissed me as minister of St. Andrew's. As Anne and I read it over, she burst into tears, and the two church men looked at her, unmoved, like she was a squashed bug.

I stared at Anderson, incredulous. For the first time, I knew that I was facing a kind of soulless violence that neither reason nor compassion could halt.

The conversation that ensued is a reflection of that violence, in all its cruel absurdity:

Anderson: "This is regrettable, but it's for your own good."
Kevin: "But why am I being fired like this? Without any review? Right out of the blue, when I had resigned already?"
Anderson: "I had to do this because of concerns that were communicated to me, in five letters from your congregation."

Kevin: "Concerns? By who?"
Silence.
Kevin: "But we have a child in school; it's winter. How can we move out of the manse right now?"
Silence.
Anne: (sobbing) "But this is so unfair. Kevin has done such good work here. A lot of people have told me how much they appreciate Kevin ..." (breaks down)
Kevin: "Forget it, Anne. That doesn't matter to him. (to Anderson) Do you like playing God?"
Anderson: "I'm not playing God. This is for your own good, and the welfare of the congregation."
Kevin: "How is it in their welfare to throw out their minister without any warning?"
Silence.
Kevin: "What am I being charged with?"
Anderson: "There are no charges against you. This isn't a disciplinary action. You're being removed for the welfare of the congregation."
Kevin: "But what is the specific reason you're firing me?"
Silence.

Anne quickly collapsed, and I took her home and spent the evening with her, huddling together in our shock like two rape victims. I was oblivious to everything else, for my world was collapsing about me.

And yet, despite this trauma, I remember that different people kept arriving at our home to try to help: an unknown native man with a large salmon, which he quietly left on our back porch; some congregants who stood around aimlessly, asking if we needed anything; members of our LIFT anti-poverty group, who wanted to picket the church to get me reinstated.

One of them who served on the church board told me that Art Anderson was meeting with the entire board at that very moment, and he had given them a statement that he insisted be read from my pulpit the following Sunday. It claimed that I was removed because I was suffering from a mental breakdown, and required "extensive

Love and Death in the Valley

psychiatric assessment and pastoral retraining". A copy of it was distributed to every member of the St. Andrew's church board.

Anderson had never made the charge of "suspected mental instability" to my face, but he was spreading that lie all over town. It was as if the lunatics had taken over the churchly asylum.

One of these crazies called me up at home that night to gloat: Phil Spencer, the secretary of Presbytery who had signed my dismissal letter. His behaviour was an example of the moral and literal madness at work within the church leadership.

Spencer was another young minister whom I had gone to school with, and who liked to joke in Presbytery meetings about his severe drinking problem. And that night, he had been on a real bender, if his incoherent tirade meant anything.

"Kevin had this coming to him!" he screamed into the phone at my mother, who had answered, and asked him why I had been fired so abruptly.

"And it's too late for you to stop us!" he ranted on. "So go ahead and sue us if you like! A lot of ministers have tried to sue the church and have never won!".

Apparently, poor Phil went on to serve as the "pastoral care" officer to other ministers in the Presbytery: a fact which proves that God really does have a sense of humour. And that churches, like fish, rot from the head down.

But despite all the cruel insanity being displayed, there was a methodical design at work in my expulsion which was identical to what was being done to Chief Earl George at the same time: **I had to be driven from the United Church and discredited at any cost, and as quickly as possible.**

This was evident in the registered letter I received just two days later from Presbytery officer Cameron Reid, which stated that I would be <u>permanently defrocked</u> as a minister unless I agreed to "psychiatric evaluation and pastoral retraining", in writing, <u>by February 9, 1995.</u>

That date was my first clue about the bigger agenda behind my firing. **<u>For February 9 was the very day that the RCMP were scheduled to open their public investigation and hearings in Port Alberni into the United Church's local Indian Residential School.</u>**

"You don't have to be a genius to see that the church wanted you out of your pulpit and silenced before the residential school dirt came out publicly" commented Bruce Gunn to me later that year. "They just had too much to lose with your open pulpit, and all those witnesses opening up to you."

Jack McDonald, a leader of the Metis Nation on Vancouver Island who attended my church, made the same comment in December, 1995 to *The Vancouver Sun*. At a protest outside the United Church head office in Vancouver, described in an article entitled *"Murders alleged at residential school"* (by Stewart Bell, December 13, 1995), McDonald told a reporter,

"We've held personal interviews with natives who were in the residential school who will tell you they carried bodies out of the school ... (We've met with) roadblock after roadblock by the United Church. They wouldn't let us see the records ... Reverend Kevin McNamee-Annett was removed last January because he was getting close to those facts, because more and more natives were opening up to him about these atrocities at the United Church."

And, at the same public protest, an eyewitness to a murder at the Alberni residential school, Harriett Nahanee, told her story for the first time of the death of little Maisie Shaw at the hands of Reverend Alfred Caldwell on Christmas eve, 1946.

With murder to conceal, the church leadership spared nothing in their frantic efforts to marginalize me.

They doctored the minutes of the St. Andrew's church board to make it appear that my congregation had requested my removal, when it was Presbytery who imposed my firing on my church. They warned everyone I knew in the United Church to stay clear of me, and circulated rumours that I had "gone crazy" and was out to destroy the church with "wild tales of atrocities". They prevented me from applying to other churches for work, threatened to fire other ministers who showed sympathy for me, and even began a smear campaign against me among the media and over the internet which is still there.

These attacks even escalated in subsequent years, as more aboriginal people came forward to corroborate my claims about crimes of the United Church, and the first major lawsuits were launched against the church by residential school survivors. But at the time of my firing, officials like Art Anderson seemed content to simply oust me from my pulpit and hope that I would wither and die in obscurity somewhere.

But my work in Port Alberni had had too deep an impact for that to happen. People began speaking out against my firing almost immediately. And their voices began to be heard in St. Andrew's church on the first Sunday after my firing.

I was too sick at heart to try entering the church that Sunday, but friends of mine did, and they describe the turmoil that seized the congregation that morning. Most people sat in shell-shocked silence, or were crying, arguing, or looking about in confusion as a clutch of Presbytery officials and Art Anderson stood at the front of the sanctuary and sternly tried conducting a "worship service".

No-one in church had been told why I was fired, beyond the obvious fabrication of "mental instability", which people laughed at when they heard. None of them knew about the secret sale of Ahousaht land, or my role in revealing it, until one of the congregants stood up to speak.

He was Nelson Keitlah, the Nuu-Chah-Nulth Tribal Council leader who had been one of the first native people to respond to my open door policy at St. Andrew's. People knew and respected him; even the Old Guard. And so the hectic mob quieted when Nelson rose with regal calmness to speak.

His words were few, and simple, but they sobered that crowd and even silenced the church officials:

Kevin was the only minister on this coast to support my people in their land claims, and now he's paying the price for it. The church abused my people, and now it's turning on its own."

When things get that clear and obvious, and the truth is spoken for all to hear, people can either face up to it, admit the wrongs, and indict the guilty—or they can choose to hide behind more lies, in which case the call goes out for the lawyers.

And that's who the United Church has continually chosen to rely on to avoid the consequences of its crimes of the past, and the present.

In my case, whenever the truth has been spoken as clearly as Nelson Keitlah did that Sunday morning, the church has responded with an elaborate mental fog and paper trail designed to hide the truth, discredit the truth-speakers, and protect the wrongdoers.

The United Church has spent millions of dollars on lawyers over the past few years, for doing the wrong thing is always more expensive than doing what's right. The church eventually doled out more than $250,000 to have me expelled from its ranks, enough money to have fed all the hungry children in Port Alberni for over two hundred years. Instead, those funds went to lawyers like Iain Benson and Jon Jessiman, the men who arranged my expulsion and the enormous smear campaign against not only me, but anyone else who spoke the truth about the church's crimes.

If only the United Church knew how to heal spiritual wounds and feed the hungry with the same expertise it employs to destroy the lives of dissidents and critics in its own ranks, it would be a powerful force for goodness in our world. But such is not the case. And that has been a hard and bitter lesson for me to learn.

Often, during the kangaroo court that expelled me from ministry the following year, I would wonder aloud why so much time and effort and money was being spent by church officials and their lawyers to get rid of one minister, when there were so many people in need of our help. It seemed so wrong, and yet the wrongness just kept plowing on over my life, with deaf ears and dead hearts.

Nelson Keitlah's words disturbed the people in St. Andrew's that morning, but they didn't change anything. The church steamroller kept flattening me and my family. I was prevented from getting work, and our funds quickly dried up.

Despite our suffering, church officials refused to negotiate or even to return my phone calls. A curtain of indifference was lowered on us, as my wife, our two little daughters and I were hung out to dry.

And yet, as things became worse for us, they also became clearer, and I found myself gaining a new trust among indigenous people who respected me for the stand I took on their behalf. My own pain and loss was bridging that chasm that separates the Two Worlds of Port Alberni, and survivors of the residential schools began sharing even more astounding evidence with me about the crimes of my church.

I met these survivors in the usual places: on the streets and in their homes, where I continued to deliver food and offer prayers after I was fired, for I carried on my ministry in Port Alberni even without a pulpit. There was nothing standing between myself and these people anymore, especially now that I shared their poverty, and the enmity of the church. And so my life became even more immersed in the struggles of those native survivors of unimaginable crimes.

During those final months in Port Alberni, until the summer of 1995, I began to systematically document the stories of murder and torture being shared with me by dozens of people. If there is such a thing as destiny, I had stumbled across part of mine. I knew that I had been put in Port Alberni to help give voice to the stories of slain and forgotten children.

And yet, at that time, I couldn't see the big picture, and the reasons the church had fired me. I still believed that a terrible mistake had been made about me by the church, and I continued to appeal to them to reinstate me.

Although penniless, and denied the right to earn my living as a minister, I went through all the steps of appeal and negotiation required by the United Church Manual—all to no avail, since every level of the church denied my appeals and upheld my arbitrary removal, even though it had never been authorized or even voted on by any proper church body.

In hindsight, this huge rubber-stamping was clear evidence of a high-level conspiracy to silence myself and other critics of the church. The crude methods used by Art Anderson and other officials to fire and "defrock" me were never once offset by conciliation or compassion by <u>anyone</u> in the United Church. Indeed, with the official blessing of the entire church leadership, Anderson was free to act with complete dishonesty and treachery from start to finish.

For example, Anderson removed me from my pulpit on January 23, 1995, in his words, "on the basis of five letters of concern" about me supposedly written to him by members of my congregation. And yet when asked to produce these letters, he refused. Nor were any such letters ever found in my personnel file or any other church record.

In fact, during my delisting trial, in the fall of 1996, <u>Anderson admitted that no such letters had ever existed;</u> that is, he had been lying to me on the day of my removal, and in fact had not received any such complaints from my parishioners! This fact alone proved not only my innocence, but Anderson's deceit; and yet

that admitted deception went unchallenged by the church officialdom, since such dishonesty is the norm in their ranks.

By June of 1995, we could not survive any longer in Port Alberni, and our family was forced to move to Vancouver, where we lived for a time with relatives. To leave Alberni felt like a personal defeat for me, but events continued to prod me towards involvement with aboriginal survivors of the residential schools.

By the time I left Alberni, the issue that had caused my expulsion had been papered over. Lot 363 was completely owned by MacMillan-Bloedel, which had established a "Joint Venture Company" with the paid-off Ahousaht band council leaders to log off the last of the old growth trees on that land. Chief Earl George had been shut out of these deals and marginalized, like me, in his own community, thanks to the aforementioned bribe of $14,000 from the very United Church officials who had had me fired. Our protests and sacrifices, it seemed, had all been in vain.

And so I was not surprised, a few years later, when MacMillan Bloedel was gobbled up by the American Multinational Weyerhauser in the biggest corporate acquisition in British Columbia's history. Lot 363 had been too tempting a morsel for this multinational and its friends in church and state, and Earl George and I had simply been in the way of the whole deal.

The whole thing broke the health of Chief George, who retired to obscurity in Port Alberni. And Bruce Gunn, the Ahousaht minister who had introduced me to Earl George, was forced from his post by the Presbytery, saw his marriage collapse under the strain, and eventually found a job as a counsellor in far-off northern B.C.

"We couldn't have won" said Bruce to me before I left for Vancouver. "There was too much money involved. So don't bother trying to negotiate with the church. They'll never let you back in after what you helped uncover. It goes even higher than you or I realise."

His words were prophetic, and borne out. And, as with my own collapsing marriage, what seemed at first like a loss, and a defeat, would actually turn out to be a blessing in disguise. For from out of these disasters came new life, and new revelations.

....

Love and Death in the Valley

MINISTER: Rev. Kevin McNamee-Annett
Telephone: 723-8332.

The letter that got me fired
— Kevin

To the Officials and Members of
Comox-Nanaimo Presbytery
The United Church of Canada

St. Andrews United Church
Port Alberni, B.C.
4574 Elizabeth Street
Port Alberni B.C.
V9Y 6L6

Dear Members of Presbytery,   17 October 1994

I am writing this in the wake of the brief discussion at the Fall Presbytery gathering in Gold River, concerning the issue of the Ahousats land settlement. I am both deeply concerned about the response of Presbytery officials to this issue, and the way in which this matter was dealt with at Presbytery.

My perspective on this issue arises largely as a result of long and fruitful discussions with the Ahousats, including with several tribal elder The issue seems to be one of violated trust on our part, rather than any legalistic or documentary problem, as Presbytery officials have suggested. In a nutshell, native land was given to the Presbyterian, and then United Church, solely for the education and spiritual upkeep of the Ahousats, in particular the young people. This land was subsequently sold by the church to a private white individual. Simple justice and decency requires that our church rectify our wrong by seeking the return of the said land to the Ahousats, and by publically admitting our mistake.

This issue has been clouded over by our Presbytery. Some officials have claimed that the Ahousats have created roadblocks to meeting, or cannot produce "appropriate" legal documentation to show ownership of the land by the Ahousats. Sadly, these are precisely the words and accusations that a colonial system has directed against indigenous peoples ever since we took away their land.

The very fact that we are waiting for the Ahousats to prove their case to us, or to meet with us on our terms, reveals at best an insensitivity on the part of our church to God's call for justice towards those we have wronged; at worst, it indicates a perpetuation of the racist and oppressive relationship that has been our legacy regarding indigenous peoples.

It is not too late to reverse this legacy, or the wrong we committed in regards to the Ahousats land issue. Indeed, it is imperative that we do so soon, if we are concerned at all about our credibility and integrity in the eyes of both the indigenous peoples here, and the wider public.

If we do not clearly and publically admit our wrong on this matter, and seek actively to return the land in question to the Ahousats people, I will find it difficult to associate myself with the United Church on this issue.

I urge Presbytery officials to meet immediately with the Ahousats elder on their terms, and come to a mutually-agreed resolution to this matter tha upholds our paper position of supporting native land claims. Anything short of this will expose a dangerous gap between our words and our actions.

Yours in Christ,
Kevin McNamee-Annett
(Rev.) Kevin McNamee-Anne

The Letter that Got Kevin Fired: His Objection to
the secret sale of Ahousaht ancestral land—'Lot 363'
by the United Church of Canada, 17 October, 1994"

TO WHOM IT MAY CONCERN:

ON JANUARY 18TH 1995 THE BOARD OF ST. ANDREW'S CHURCH ACCEPTED REVEREND KEVIN McNAMEE - ANNETT'S RESIGNATION. AT THAT TIME THE BOARD'S DECISION WAS TO KEEP REVEREND KEVIN McNAMEE- ANNETT AS MINISTER OF ST. ANDREWS CHURCH UNTIL THE END OF JUNE 1995. ALSO KEVIN AND HIS FAMILY COULD STAY IN ST. ANDREWS HOUSE FOR THE SAME PERIOD OF TIME.

WHEN PRESBYTER CAME TO THE NEXT MEETING THEY STATED THAT THEY WERE NOW LOOKING AFTER THE DECISION'S REGARDING REVEREND KEVIN McNAMEE- ANNETT AND THAT THE DECISION'S MADE BY ST. ANDREW'S BOARD WERE NOT GOING TO BE FOLLOWED. THEY STATED THAT KEVIN WAS TO BE REMOVED AS MINISTER IMMEDIATELY AND PASSED AROUND A DOCUMENT WHICH STATED THIS FACT. THE BOARD WAS TOLD NOT TO DIVULGE ANY OF THIS INFORMATION TO KEVIN.

ALL MATTERS CONCERNING KEVIN McNAMEE ANNETT WERE HANDLED BY PRESBYTER. THE SPOKESPERSON FOR PRESBYTER WAS A MR. REID.

THESE FACTS ARE TRUE AS I REMEMBER THEM.

GERRY WALERIUS   AUGUST 26, 1996

Gerry Walerius (signature)

The Covert Removal of Kevin after his Objection - Affidavit of Gerry Walerius, former Board Member at St. Andrew's United Church, Port Alberni, 26 August, 1996

Love and Death in the Valley

CITY & REGION

Murders alleged at residential school

NDP leadership candidate claims 2 Indians killed in Port Alberni in '40s and '50s.

STEWART BELL
Vancouver Sun

At least two students were murdered at Indian residential schools in the Port Alberni area in the 1940s and '50s, a candidate for the leadership of the New Democratic Party alleged Tuesday.

Jack McDonald, who led a demonstration outside the United Church offices in Vancouver to protest the church's treatment of aboriginal people, called for a public inquiry into the deaths.

However, the head of an RCMP probe investigating abuse at Indian residential schools says he knows nothing about the allegations.

"To me that's a totally new allegation, and I'm familiar with all the information that's come in from Port Alberni," said Sgt. Paul Willms.

"I haven't even heard a rumor or second-hand information of that nature."

McDonald said former students at residential schools in Port Alberni and nearby Ahousaht have recently come forward with stories about the deaths.

In one case, a boy is said to have bled to death after he was beaten as punishment for breaking a jar at the school in Ahousaht in the '40s.

A second death is said to have occurred in the early 50s, when a girl was kicked down a flight of stairs at the Alberni Indian Residential School.

"We've held personal interviews with natives who were in the residential school who will tell you they carried bodies out of the school," said McDonald.

The incidents could not be found in police or coroners' records and attempts to research the alleged deaths were met with "roadblock after roadblock" by the United Church, he said.

"They wouldn't let us see the records," said McDonald, a Port Alberni funeral planner who is the only declared candidate so far for Premier Mike Harcourt's job.

He also said the United Church removed Rev. Kevin McNamee-Annett from Port Alberni last January because he was "getting close to those facts, because more and more natives were opening up to him about these atrocities at the United Church."

McDonald wants Attorney-General Ujjal Dosanjh and Aboriginal Affairs Minister John Cashore to order a public inquiry and police investigation.

Art Anderson, personnel minister for the B.C. conference of the United Church, said the church is cooperating fully with the police investigation into residential schools.

He said he invited the demonstrators to his office to discuss their concerns, which they did. "There's no attempt to dodge communication or hide anything."

Anderson said he was unable to comment on the reasons for McNamee-Annett's dismissal. "That matter is before the church courts so it would be inappropriate to discuss that at the moment."

McNamee-Annett said the stories about the killings were told to him while he was working with Nuu-chah-nulth Indians in the Alberni Valley.

He said he will not reveal the names of the victims.

But he said he had urged the witnesses to take their accounts to authorities.

In a letter to McNamee-Annett dated Nov. 15, the head of human rights and aboriginal justice for the United Church of Canada called the murder allegations "deeply disturbing."

"If you have evidence related to such allegations, I trust you have reported this to the appropriate police authorities and will encourage others to do so as well," wrote John Siebert.

"It is worth repeating that the United Church of Canada fully supports the investigation of any and all criminal actions alleged to have taken place in residential schools."

Siebert said in an interview from Toronto Tuesday he isn't aware what requests have been made for documents related to the Alberni Valley schools, but he doubts they would be useful in investigating abuse.

"These are records that probably aren't going to record these kinds of stories from the aboriginal people's perspective," he said.

Willms suggested it may be that former students are now recalling deaths that were ruled accidental at the time. He said the deaths would certainly fall within the mandate of the police investigation.

The RCMP formed the probe almost a year ago to investigate allegations that large numbers of Indian children were sexually and physically abused at church-run schools.

Beginning in the 1880s, Indian children were removed, sometimes forcibly, from their homes and sent to residential schools in an attempt to assimilate them.

The policy was abandoned in the '70s, but the lingering effects of residential school abuse are blamed for a variety of ills on Indian reserves, including high rates of suicide, substance abuse and family breakdown.

CENTRE OF PROTEST: Rev. Kevin McNamee-Annett details allegations

The Vancouver Sun, Wednesday, December 13, 1995

The First Public Allegations of Murder at Alberni Residential School,
The Vancouver Sun, 13 December, 1995

Kevin Annett

Some of the letters of support for Kevin Annett
from his parish members which were never included in
the church's 'official delisting' report on him, 1995-1996

THE PORT ALBERNI METIS ASSOCIATION

\# 51 - 4110 Kendall Avenue
Port Alberni, B.C.
V9Y 5J1

Phone (604) 723-2892
Fax   (604) 724-1171

PROUD TO BE METIS

May 8, 1995

The British Columbia Conference
of the United Church
Vancouver, B.C.

To Whom It May Concern:

    The Metis people of Port Alberni were extremely upset upon witnessing the actions of the United Church of British Columbia against the one man of God who was responsible for touching the lives of many of our people. Reverend Kevin McNamee-Annett has been the one ray of hope that we have experienced in our community. Your actions to destroy his work and reputation is nothing less than criminal.

The Metis people have undergone years of persecution fighting for their rights and all during this time have experienced many injustices and criminal acts against our people by the same type of individuals who now attack Reverend McNammee-Annett.

This man of God, was the one person in our community who gave us a clear understanding of our relationship with God. He showed us that there are three components to a balanced relationship; respect, equity, and empowerment. We learned that if we take lots of respect, and have little equity and no empowerment, then we are treated like children. If we are given a little bit of respect, with lots of equity and no empowerment, then we are treated like prostitutes. If we are given lots of empowerment, with little equity and little respect, then we are treated like police officers. It was Reverend McNammee-Annett who helped us to see and experbence God so that we had adequate amounts of respect, equity, and empowerment.

The Metis people will ensure that your actions against Reverend McNammee-Annett are made public and that our childrens, childrens, children never forget the actions of the United Church against a man of God, who was loved by our people.

Sincerely,

Jack McDonald

Jack McDonald
President

Love and Death in the Valley

July 2, 1996

To Whom it May Concern,

I first attended services led by Kevin Annett in the summer of 1993 during my frequent visits to family in Port Alberni. Although I was a member of the United Church in Vancouver, Kevin's services with their messages of tolerance, love and action touched a chord with me that no other minister's had. So when my first child was born in the fall of 1993 I asked Kevin to baptise her in his church in Port Alberni. Kevin's messages seemed to me to be the closest to the spirit of the words of Jesus and true Christianity. We cannot be complacent in a world filled with unjustice and we have a responsibility to help those less fortunate than ourselves. It seemed to my husband and I that it was this spirit that motivated all Kevin's words and actions and we have the greatest respect and admiration for him. It takes courage to stand up for the poor and dispossessed against the wealthy and the powerful but that is what Kevin does again and again. The world needs more people like him.

Yours truly,

Clodagh and Jay Scott
#23-717 W. 8th Avenue,
Vancouver, B.C.
V5Z 1C9
(604) 879 1298

Kevin Annett

Chapter Three: Learning to Speak the Unspeakable—A Funeral, An Inquisition and a Tribunal

"The residential school was just like the rest of the world: you learned at a young age that there's things you talk about and things you never talk about, or you get hammered."
Harvey Brooks, survivor, Alberni Indian Residential School, June 12, 1998

"There are rules in any organization, and Kevin forgot the rules. When he said he had to put God first, he was being pastorally incompetent."
Bob Stiven, Comox-Nanaimo Presbytery official, October 8, 1996

"Certain people are getting very upset about what you've been saying about children being killed at the residential schools, and they may take action to stop you."
RCMP Sgt. Paul Willms to Kevin Annett, June 24, 1996

When our little family drove out of the Alberni valley for the last time, on a clear June day in 1995, I thought I'd never see the place again, except perhaps on summer excursions to the west coast beaches. And yet, within a few months, I was called back to Port Alberni to conduct a funeral, and help launch the first public inquiry into coastal residential schools; an inquiry whose impetus was that funeral.

My family and I had just settled into student housing at the University of British Columbia, where I had enrolled in a doctoral native studies program, when I received a collect phone call from John Sargent, a homeless man in Port Alberni who had come to know me well at St. Andrew's.

"You'd better get your ass up here, Kev" John announced. "Cecilia Joseph just burned to death in a slum fire."

It was devastating news. Cecilia was a quiet, friendly woman from Ahousaht whom I had befriended at our Loaves and Fishes food bank. She had arrived one Wednesday morning to collect a bag of groceries for her family, and stayed the rest of the day, helping to bag food and carry kids, and talking to me about her life.

Cecilia once showed me the scars on her arms and legs from the long needles that nuns had shoved into her as a little girl, at the Catholics' Christie residential school near Tofino. And she had seen a five year old cousin beaten to death by a priest at the same school.

Cecilia Joseph, too, died horribly on the morning of September 5, 1995. The one room she rented from Alberni slum landlord Gus Frigstad lacked a door handle and fire alarms, so she was unable to escape when the building caught fire. The local fire department took a half hour to arrive, and by then Cecilia was dead.

I was asked by her family to conduct her funeral. But no church in Port Alberni would allow the service to take place on their premises.

The Ambroses, Cecilia's wider family, had phoned every church in the Alberni Valley by the time I arrived in town on September 6, but when the local clergy discovered who the funeral was for, they all refused to let us use their buildings, whether Protestant, Catholic or evangelical.

That included both United Churches in town. The new minister at St. Andrew's, Kathleen Hogman—whom I had never met, but who would later be one of the church's "witnesses" against me at my defrocking trial—claimed the sanctuary was being used at the time we needed it, which turned out not to be true. But the more blatant response came from Ryan Knight, the minister at First United church; another former classmate and friend of mine who had cut off all contact with me immediately after I was fired.

When Cecilia's brother asked Ryan for the use of his church for her funeral, Ryan replied, "That's not possible, if Kevin is the minister conducting the service. He's in deep trouble with the church and is not allowed to use any United Church facility."

That was a new lie, but it kept Indians out of Ryan's church, which was his main objective. For, according to Cecilia's brother, "That's not the first time he's turned us down. Our grandparents tried to have our kids baptised at that church and that same minister said no to them. He told them that Indians who wanted help or baptisms had to go to the Native Pentecostal Church."

Nobody de-segregates Port Alberni very easily. The fact that I was able to do so at St. Andrew's clearly set off alarm bells among the "white" establishment in town, and their kept clergy, like Ryan, with sad consequences for Cecilia and her family.

Eventually, we were able to book the local Odd Fellows Hall for her funeral, and over a hundred people crammed into its basement the next day to do homage to Cecilia, and remember how she died.

That wasn't all that was remembered. Cecilia's funeral suddenly became a public witnessing to the suffering of other Indians in the valley, past and present. And that is where our investigation into the residential school crimes really began.

As I always had done from my pulpit, I opened up the service to anyone who wished to speak. One of the Ambrose relatives, an older man who leaned on a cane, stood up shakily and thundered, "Our dear Cecilia wouldn't have hurt a fly, but look at how she died. She was just another innocent victim. I'm sick of so many of our people dying like this. Nothing's changed since the residential school days. We all saw our friends raped and killed there by evil men like Principal Caldwell, and he got away with it, just like Frigstad has gotten away with murdering Cecilia. We can't let this thing happen anymore."

The old man's words were the first time that a suspected murderer of children at the Alberni residential school had been publicly named. His bravery cracked open the wall of silence, and others stood up to name their rapists, and other killers.

After several hours, exhausted yet elated, many of the mourners began to leave the hall. But ten or so people lingered, and they began discussing how to honour Cecilia's memory with more than a single service. This group was the seed out of which the subsequent inquiries and Tribunals into west coast residential schools emerged.

Several of the founders of this group had worked with me at St. Andrew's in the LIFT anti-poverty group, and one of them, Jack McDonald of the local Metis Society, proposed that we hold a "Citizens' Inquiry into Crimes Against Humanity on Vancouver Island". The idea behind this was to create a public forum in which witnesses to the atrocities at the residential schools could speak out in safety and have their stories documented. We hoped to then send the evidence to the Human Rights Commission of the United Nations.

This idea spread like wildfire in the local native communities, through the "moccasin telegraph", and soon Jack and I were receiving

Love and Death in the Valley

a dozen or more calls every week from survivors who had grisly and never-told stories to share.

One of these tales even made it into the Vancouver Sun that December, as its bearer, elder Archie Frank from Ahousaht, described seeing a young boy named Albert Gray beaten to death by the same Principal, Alfred Caldwell, who had been named at our gathering for killing another child at the Alberni school. (see *"Beaten to Death for Theft of a Prune"* by Mark Hume, The Vancouver Sun, December 20, 1995, below)

Cecilia's funeral was another trigger in the power-keg that is Port Alberni. Even in death, Cecilia kept serving her people; for opened mouths are much harder to close than a church food bank, or a minister's job.

Our Citizens' Inquiry opened in early December of 1995, and it issued summonses to the heads of the government, churches, and corporations like MacMillan-Bloedel to answer charges of murder, land theft and planned genocide. As at the larger Tribunal held over two years later in Vancouver under United Nations auspices, none of the officials subpoenaed ever responded, and the media spread a blackout over our work. But the stories began to be told, and recorded.

In response to the media disinterest in the most important story in Canadian history, we decided to do a more dramatic public action to gain some attention. And so we organized a protest and picket line outside the United Church's head office in Vancouver on December 12, 1995.

I suppose I do believe in fate, of a sort, because at that chilly protest I first met Harriett Nahanee, another witness to murder at the Alberni residential school. And I knew quickly that she and I were meant to meet.

When she was ten years old, on Christmas Eve in 1946, Harriett was hiding in her usual haven under the stairs of the girls' dormitory in the Alberni residential school. It was the only place she could escape from Alfred Caldwell, the school Principal, who along with a staff member named Edward Peake, raped and beat Harriett whenever he pleased. It was from this spot that she saw Caldwell murder fourteen year old Maisie Shaw from Port Renfrew.

"She was crying for her mother at the top of the stairs" Harriett recalls. "I heard her being yelled at by Caldwell and a matron, a Welsh lady who always carried a thick strap on her belt. Then I heard him kick Maisie and she came flying down those stairs. I'll never forget that awful thud. I looked out and she was lying on the floor, not moving, with her eyes wide open. Then her body disappeared, and no-one ever saw her again."

Harriett, like Archie Frank, shared her story with the <u>Vancouver Sun</u> (*"Claim of murder goes back to '40's"* by Karen Gram, December 18, 1995, below). But before she did, she told me her story on the day after we met, at her home in North Vancouver. She was sitting under a gallery of photographs of her children, and grandchildren, for Harriett was over 60 at the time, and every year of weary struggle was etched on her wrinkled face.

She spoke of her early years, of watching every child in her west coast village of Clo-ose grabbed and hauled away by RCMP officers to the Alberni residential school, of being hidden by relatives until she was ten, when the Mounties finally caught her. She recounted being held down by a white dentist at the residential school, who drilled her teeth and pulled them out without administering painkillers. She named friends of hers who were beaten to death and buried in the woods behind the school, or sterilised by church doctors, or farmed out to wealthy pedophiles and never seen again.

After a few hours of such horror stories, I broke in and asked Harriett, "So what was it all about?"

She looked at me almost disdainfully, and barked,

"We were the Keepers of the Land; that is the special job given to our people by Creator. And the whites wanted the land, the trees and the fish. So they had to brainwash us to forget we had to guard and preserve the land for our Creator. That's why they put us in the residential schools, and terrorized us, so we'd forget our language and our laws, and allow the land to be stolen. And it worked. The whites have 99% of the land now, and our people are dying off. That's why it's never been about God, or 'civilizing' us. It's always been about the land."

Harriett became a guide for me into the Holocaust that claimed most of her people, at the same time that I was uncovering more archival evidence that would help her and other school survivors successfully sue the United Church.

Harriett was the one who introduced me to many of the survivors who live in Vancouver. Together, we founded a "Circle of Justice" the following year, which moved people beyond simply participating in healing circles to publicly challenging the government and the churches over their planned genocide of native nations. And, as part of my doctoral research, I kept discovering documents and letters in the University of BC Library's archives which implicated men like Alfred Caldwell in the crimes Harriett and others testified to personally.

United Church officials were well aware of all this, and it worried them greatly; so much so that the very day after our protest outside the church office, on December 14, 1995, Brian Thorpe, the church official who had instigated my firing, contacted my wife, Anne McNamee, and urged her to begin the divorce action against me that she had been planning since the previous spring, in conjunction with himself and church lawyer Jon Jessiman.

Anne knew that I was facing permanent defrocking long before I did, since Jessiman and Thorpe had told her so, and that was enough to push her towards divorcing me. As I mentioned, earlier, she and her lawyer timed her divorce action to coincide with the church's agenda; thus, the day after our protest was reported in *The Vancouver Sun*, she told me she was leaving me. Two weeks later, she stole away with our children, and had court papers served on me.

All of this came out during our divorce trial, which occurred at precisely the same time as the church's "delisting" procedures against me. Again, this was no coincidence. Anne and her lawyer were very open about how they had worked with United Church officials like Phil Spencer and Brian Thorpe to plan the details of the divorce, and obtain "incriminating" evidence on me; like my personal journal, which Anne stole off my computer one night while I still lived with her.

Even the church admitted their sordid actions. According to Rev. Bruce Gunn, who was present, the Treasurer of my former Presbytery, Colin Forbes, announced publicly at their regular meeting in February, 1996 that unforeseen expenses "related to the Kevin

McNamee-Annett case" had occurred as a result of "our lawyer meeting with Kevin's wife, Anne, on several occasions this month".
(from an affidavit of July 3, 1996)

All of these sick little plots seemed so bizarre when I first heard them admitted in divorce court that I couldn't believe it. But the Presbytery documents in the hands of Anne's lawyer weren't imagined. The church, it seems, became so worried about me once I teamed up with Harriett Nahanee and other eyewitnesses to the Alberni murders that it sunk to any level to destroy my effectiveness and my spirit, including by tying me up in a messy and heart-breaking divorce that took my children away from me.

People who hear this story tend to immediately ask me, in horror, "But how can Christians act like that?". I usually respond by saying, "Those weren't Christians, they were church officials."

But I also ask them to know their own history. For when have such lies and cruelty ever been alien to the Christian church? What the "official Christians" did to Jews, women, Indigenous peoples and dissidents for many centuries they are now practising on one another—even on their own clergy and their families. That fact alone should tell us something.

Be that as it may, it quickly became clear to me that, while church officers like Brian Thorpe and Jon Jessiman originally fired me in order to conceal the Ahousaht land deal, they arranged my subsequent "delisting" from ministry in the same kind of panic-reaction, in response to the efforts of Harriett Nahanee and I to publicly expose the evidence of murder and cover-up at the Alberni residential school.

Once again, the church admitted this during the kangaroo court that expelled me from ministry the following year. The church lawyer, a weasly little guy named Iain Benson, stated on the opening day of the hearing,

"We are satisfied that Reverend Annett complied with Presbytery's original demands on him. We are recommending his delisting now not because of his Port Alberni ministry, but because of recent matters of behaviour on his part involving his accusations about the death of native children in the church's residential schools."

By their own admission, I was being thrown out of my profession for a single reason: because I had spoken out publicly about children who had died in the church's residential schools, <u>not</u> because I wasn't a good minister!

In fact, it was just <u>two days</u> after the first group of Alberni residential school survivors began their class action lawsuit against the United Church, in early February, 1996, that Presbytery officials voted to recommend "delisting" me from ministry, without giving any reason.

We live in a cynical culture deluged with "conspiracy theories"; an obsession caused, perhaps, by the background radiation of fear that hums through our lives. And so it is a natural reaction to deny conspiracy when we encounter it, especially when it comes close to home. Maybe that's why I didn't recognise what was happening to me, at first. But within a year of my firing, I was forced to explain why the United Church was spending so much time, and money, to drive one minister—me—from its ranks, while simultaneously claiming that I had done nothing wrong and faced no charges whatsoever.

My circumstances, and fate, were clearer to other people than to myself, especially people who had known similar, and worse, punishment at the hands of the same church. People like Harriett Nahanee.

"It's only white people who can't believe that the church killed children" she commented to me one day. "You don't even know your own history. How many people have the Christians killed? More than any religion on earth. What was another Indian, to them? Or another minister who got too close to the murders, like you did?"

I recognized all that, abstractly. But it wasn't until my "delisting" trial, in the fall of 1996, that the pieces in the church's jig-saw began to fall into place for me.

I should first explain how unusual was the church's move to "delist" me. That's a typically antiseptic term which means stripping a minister of his ordination and livelihood. There had never been a public delisting of a United Church minister in history before mine. Obviously, there has to be a pretty strong reason for delisting, since it prevents a professional from ever again practising his or her career. But in my case, there was no reason given.

It was one thing to remove me from my pulpit; but the church wanted to throw me right out of its ranks. That made absolutely no sense, even by their self-serving logic, since the church claimed that I had been fired "for the peace and welfare" of the St. Andrew's congregation, **not because I was generally unfit as a minister.**

No, the church didn't dare to make such a claim until I began speaking out publicly with Harriett about the deaths of children at the Alberni residential school, more than one year after my firing. Then my fate was sealed.

Absurdly, the church was never able to prove that I was unfit as a minister, but I was delisted anyway: without first-hand evidence, or the chance to face my accusers or be tried by my peers, or any of the other rights I thought I enjoyed as a citizen of Canada. But the church, I learned, is a law unto itself, and beyond the law of our land—something any native person could have told me long before my legal lynching by the "official Christians".

Imagine entering a courtroom after having been arrested for no stated reason. You're not told why you're there and you can't see your accusers or know the charges against you. But you have to somehow convince a judge and a jury of three people, who are all from the same church executive body, why they shouldn't expel you from your profession. And you have to do so without a lawyer, and without knowing the court's procedures, while your adversary—who is also from the same church body as the judge and jury—has legal representation and millions of dollars at his disposal, and you are penniless.

Finally, to complete this nightmare, the judge himself (Jon Jessiman) was the lawyer for your adversary, still gives them legal advice, has made disparaging comments about you in court, goes to lunch and hobnobs with the jury, and confers with them and your adversary's lawyer in private. And the man who appointed the jury (Brian Thorpe) is the same guy who arranged your "arrest" in the first place, has

disparaged you in public and throughout the church, and is now called as a primary witness against you!

This was the United Church "hearing", and process, that deprived me of my life's calling. Anywhere else, it's known for what it is: a kangaroo court. Or, more accurately, a legal lynching.

"Kevin's trial was a failed attempt at cosmetics" wrote an observer of the hearing to BC's then Attorney-General, Ujjal Dosanjh, after my delisting. "There was no due process of any kind. It was a simple railroading masked to look like a legitimate hearing."

Twenty-four other observers of the charade thought so too, and they also petitioned the Attorney-General to investigate my trial. But Dosanjh—a cabinet colleague and self-described "good friend" of United Church clergyman John Cashore, who brokered the Lot 363 deal and probably had me fired, and who later ran Dosanjh's NDP leadership campaign—refused to do so.

The fact that mine was the first public delisting of a United Church minister in history revealed the purpose of the whole thing. Usually, the railroading process occurs behind closed doors in the church; but in my case, the world, and church members in particular, were encouraged to witness my professional cashiering. My public crucifixion was designed as a warning to other, potentially dissident clergy and church members. It's for that reason that I see my delisting not simply as having been a "kangaroo court", but a **show trial**.

A tremendous amount was at stake for the United Church in my case: not only had their own officials violated my rights under both the law and their own Manual, but they had done so with a clear and obvious intent to silence a whistle-blower—someone who had revealed "club secrets": the church's illegal sale of native land to its corporate friends, the complicity of government ministers like John Cashore in that sale and its concealment, and of course the first evidence of murder and other crimes against native children at United Church facilities.

Wouldn't any big company consider such a threat worth spending $250,000 to contain and cover-up? And, with assets exceeding $4 billion, the United Church of Canada is nothing if not a large corporation.

By the fall of 1996, when my delisting trial began, the church feared that it stood to lose most of those assets in lawsuits brought by its aboriginal victims, which leapt in number from a few dozen to thousands in a short time. The whole issue of residential schools was no longer just an abstract topic of conversation: it threatened to destroy the church, at least in the minds of its officials. To quote Brian Thorpe, "We knew we had to do something quickly after Kevin wrote his letter, and began speaking about murders". *(to the Conference sub-Executive, March, 1997)*

Essentially, the United Church had committed so many wrongs that there was only one way to deal with them, in the minds of company-men like Thorpe and Jessiman: to completely discredit and destroy the person who had surfaced the wrongs in the first place. Nothing else can explain what the church did to me, and what it continues to do in the wake of my "delisting".

....

The year after I was expelled from the United Church, their officials proved my allegations by finally admitting to the press that they had engaged in covering up evidence of crimes at its Alberni residential school since at least 1960, in league with the federal government. (*"see Church-school victim got no help"*, below)

I consider my firing and expulsion from ministry to have been part of this decades-long effort by the church to deny and bury the truth of its crimes. I am simply one of the most recent, and public, victims of this cover-up campaign.

Step One in my victimisation had been accomplished through my firing and denial of work in the church. Step Two in this sorry charade began on August 28, 1996, with the commencement of my public defrocking as a minister.

It took place in a church, naturally, and the proceedings opened with prayer. Even Cardinal Richelieu used to pray for his victims. But after that formality, God checked out for good.

The trial was deceptively arranged to resemble a legitimate court of law. Jon Jessiman, who had been the lawyer for Presbytery against me, now wore the hat of judge! (No kidding). Beside him sat three long-time church officials, all of them hand-picked by Jessiman's

Love and Death in the Valley

partner in my firing, Brian Thorpe, who was later called as a witness against me. And Comox-Nanaimo Presbytery, which had brought on the motion to delist me, was represented by a right-wing Catholic lawyer named Iain Benson, who eventually took more than $58,000 from the United Church for his efforts to expel me.

I had no legal representation, no money, and no information on the guidelines of the trial. The church, and specifically Brian Thorpe, had repeatedly refused to provide me with the charges against me, the names of my accusers, the reasons for my firing and recommended defrocking, or even the grounds for de-listing a minister.

Those facts alone should have nullified the whole process then and there. But the church was writing its own arbitrary rules as it went along, and expecting me to operate by them.

I refused to do so from the start, asking at the very beginning of the trial for a list of the charges against me and the grounds for delisting a minister: information which was mine to receive under Canadian law and natural justice.

This request for fair treatment, naturally, created disorder. The chairperson of the delisting panel, a neatly-dressed minister named Mollie Williams, became quite upset at my request, and she had to huddle with Judge Jessiman for a few moments. (The two of them knew each other well; she had nominated Jessiman for Moderator of the United Church years before).

Miss Mollie emerged from their conference looking relieved, but her words were astounding. Like a machine, she repeated quickly, "There are no charges against you. This hearing is called in response to a request by Comox-Nanaimo Presbytery that your name be struck from the Active Service List of ministers. There are no stated criteria for delisting a minister in the United Church. You will have to provide those criteria to the panel yourself, but the actual criteria will be determined by the panel only at the end of this hearing."

There it was, in all its black and white absurdity: I was not charged with anything, but I was facing expulsion from the ministry anyway, and I couldn't know what grounds I was being expelled on! Incredibly, those grounds would be established only <u>after</u> the hearing, when my chance to speak and respond was gone!

How, then, could I conduct any kind of defense of myself?

Clearly, I couldn't. And I said so to Miss Mollie. Caught off guard, she blinked, and looked at Jessiman helplessly.

The double talk that spewed from the lawyer's mouth would have impressed any politician, but of course it answered nothing. Reality kept being reinvented by him, or, in the words of one observer, "He just kept moving the goal posts around". That became the standard procedure for this tragedy that quickly became farce.

Take the matter of witnesses and evidence, for example. Citing "rules of procedure", Jessiman said that no hearsay evidence was allowed. And yet the Presbytery lawyer, Iain Benson, proceeded to call four witnesses against me who had no first-hand experience of either me or my ministry. One of them, in fact, had never even met me! And yet Benson was allowed to base his entire case against me on such hearsay evidence, without objection from Judge Jessiman.

A different standard applied when it came to my turn. Jessiman curtly cut me off whenever I strayed into "hearsay", while Benson was allowed to ask his witnesses questions like "What is it that you heard about Kevin?", and so on, without a peep from Jessiman.

This gross double-standard and prejudice at work against me became so absurdly obvious, so quickly, that many of the observers at the hearing began laughing, shaking their heads, and leaving the room in despair. One of them, a retired policeman from Victoria, came over to me and asked, "Why are you taking part in this kangaroo court, son?"

I kept wondering the same thing myself. But underneath all my doubts and anger at being subjected once again to blind injustice, I kept struggling to discover what the church's agenda towards me actually was. Why was I being driven out of the United Church, and maligned so badly along the way?

The answer began revealing itself the longer I persisted in the hearing, and that made the whole ordeal worthwhile.

One of my best allies in this search for the truth was the very arrogance and self-confidence of the church, and its witnesses against me. Two of the latter blurted out some things that clearly indicated the bigger agenda behind my removal, to the great chagrin of Jessiman.

Their names were Bob Stiven and Win Stokes, two sad-looking Presbytery officials who had played a big role in my secret firing from St. Andrew's. Their involvement in that sordid affair clearly didn't sit well with them; unlike Jessiman, they seemed to retain some shreds of conscience, and could not look directly at me as they sat in the witness chair and answered Iain Benson's leading questions.

Stiven is a short, wiry-haired Scotsman whom I had met maybe twice before the hearing. He had never been to my Port Alberni church during my ministry there, and never heard me preach a sermon. But it seems that somehow he was an expert about me, and his passionate disapproval of my reaching out to native people verged on racism.

"Kevin spent all his time concerned about other people than the gray-haired English grannies who are the backbone of our church" Stiven spouted, to guffaws in the audience. When he heard those reactions, he turned red and nearly shouted,

"Laugh if you like, but there's no way Kevin had a future in our Presbytery. Not with all that social justice stuff he was preaching."

The room went silent, and Jessiman looked like he was about to have a coronary. He actually hurried over to Benson, the Presbytery's lawyer, and conferred with him. Benson then quickly asked Stiven, "But wouldn't you say that Reverend Annett received a fair treatment in the courts of our church?"

Stiven was not on track, clearly, and the poor guy was so worked into a lather that he couldn't catch the lawyer's intent, and his obvious concern about Stiven's last remark. The Scotsman blurted out,

"Look, in my rage, I doubt if Kevin would have received a fair hearing in the Presbytery. Not after he started talking about all those dead Indian children."

The church had just lost its case against me, I figured. I was elated at this admission from one of its own officers that I faced a prejudiced employer unwilling to give myself or my ministry a fair hearing. Stiven had just revealed some of the hidden agenda: the Presbytery guys wanted an "Injun lover" out of their territory!

Jessiman obviously realised this, too, for he immediately closed the hearing for an extended recess. When things reconvened, an hour later, he instructed the panel to disregard Stiven's statements, on the grounds that they were "not relevant" to the issue of my "suitability for ministry"!

I challenged his ruling, naturally. I asked Jessiman how the way that Presbytery officials—my employers—regarded me was "not relevant" to my ministering, since I operated in a broader context of serving as a member of the Presbytery: a fact that the church lawyer himself kept going on about.

Jessiman responded by questioning my motives and disparaging me. Like they teach you in law school, when the evidence isn't on your side, you attack the witness. But it isn't often the case in a supposed court of law that the judge gets to function as the prosecuting attorney, like Big Jon was doing.

In this way, Judge Jessiman kept steering the trial away from anything that would detract from Presbytery's fabricated case against me—that I was an "unfit" minister—and from any evidence that implicated the church in other scandals, like the selling of native land to its corporate benefactor, the logging multinational MacMillan-Bloedel.

Unfortunately for Jessiman, the other witness I mentioned, Win Stokes, shot the church in the foot over precisely such a scandal: the Ahousaht land deal.

Stokes was even more nervous than Bob Stiven; he kept wiping his face and moving about in his chair under my stare. He had been the liaison person between Presbytery and the higher church officials who had engineered my secret removal.

Desperate to undo the damage that Stiven's words had made on their case, Benson asked Stokes to describe the process of my removal from St. Andrew's, probably to show justification for it all. But Stokes was too honest in his answer.

"Well, the thing is that we had no concerns about Kevin at all until he wrote his letter about the Ahousaht's land claim, in October of 1994" Stokes answered matter-of-factly. But he froze when he saw the look of anguish on Benson's face.

Making matters worse for his lawyer, Stokes blundered on.

"I mean, that's the first time I heard of Kevin. Speaking personally ... Well, it's just that a senior government official told me that we couldn't let Kevin upset the applecart over Lot 363."

Angrily, "Judge" Jessiman immediately jumped in and shut Stokes down.

"This is not relevant to Presbytery's line of questioning" he announced, once again playing the role of prosecutor. He recessed the hearing and conferred with Benson and the panel for over an hour.

I don't know why Win Stokes mentioned the "senior government minister", undoubtedly John Cashore, and his role in my firing. Perhaps he wanted to save his own neck, and justify Presbytery's actions by sharing the blame a bit. But once again, I and many others that day were convinced that the church had just lost its case against me. **For Stokes had confessed that I was removed from St. Andrew's not because of my "unsuitability" as a minister, but because I had written a letter about the Ahousaht land deal.**

When Jessiman and his cronies returned, the damage-control set in. Stokes was excused from the witness stand and Jessiman gave a long lecture about what was "irrelevant" to the hearing: namely, anything that related to my ministry with natives, or issues pertaining to the Ahousaht land deal or the residential schools! The panel was even ordered by him to "disregard" any testimony about these things.

In so doing, Jon Jessiman exposed not only the agenda of the church, and his own role in it—to keep their wrongdoing hidden—but he invalidated himself as an impartial or competent judge. I asked the panel that they remove him as the adjudicator of the hearing because of my "perception of bias" in him.

Miss Mollie ruled my motion "out of order". The farce carried on.

When Jessiman announced that my "suitability" for ministry could not be determined by any reference to my ministry with native people, he was doing more than covering for the residential school crimes, or the land deals: he was faithfully repeating the Christian Imperial attitude that Indians are ultimately of no account. I was surprised at how clearly Jessiman was incriminating himself, and the church as a whole, in the very supremacist ideology that had killed off more than 50,000 Indian children in the residential schools. But I was even more amazed at how easily he was able to get away with it all.

I responded to Jessiman's ruling by ignoring it. I continued to ask questions and present evidence related to my full ministry in Port Alberni—including with aboriginal people, since that had formed so much of what I had done there—and how I had built up my congregation to more than three times its original number, and had maintained it at that level until the day of my firing.

Jessiman and the panel really began to hate me after that, and they showed it. Big Jon let slip comments like "We've come to expect this from Kevin"—a fairly impartial comment from a "judge", don't you think?—and threatened to clear the room of all observers and place the proceedings "in camera" on several occasions.

But his main counter-offensive came in the form of the next witness for Presbytery, his fellow stage-manager of my firing, "Lyin' Brian" Thorpe: the top United Church officer in BC at the time, and now a national official of the church.

Thorpe is like the crooked police chief in gangster movies who sets up a hit and then stands back to cover for the criminals with a beneficent smile on his face.

It was Thorpe who had been called in as a "fireman" to put out the Lot 363 crisis for the church, after I wrote my letter. He had then engineered my removal, paid off Ahousaht band councillors to distance themselves from Chief Earl George, and arranged similar bribes to tribal chiefs in Port Alberni to isolate myself and Earl. And now he was to "testify" about me to the panel!

Thorpe's manner is so bland and gentle that no-one would suspect him of being the unscrupulous hatchet-man that he is. He was called by the church as its next witness to undo the testimonies of Stokes and Stiven, and place on record the church's official "line" about the scandals raised in the hearing.

But even Thorpe ended up incriminating the church, and strengthening my legitimacy as a minister.

Once again, over-confidence let things slip. Thorpe was so determined to present himself as a nice guy, removed from the obvious racism and prejudices of the Presbytery officials, that he proved my case.

When asked to respond to the allegation that I had been fired for my ministry with native people, Thorpe chuckled and said, "No, Kevin was not special. He was doing what many of our ministers do. Others have said and done far more controversial things in the church than Kevin."

Thorpe is no dummy, and he realised how that one strengthened me. After all, if I was so similar to other "social justice" oriented ministers in the church, then why were Thorpe and company spending so much time and money throwing me out? So he added quickly, "In the kingdom of God, there will be no injustice, no rich or poor. I think Kevin's only mistake was to think that could happen now, and he didn't make the compromises we all have to do to stay in the church."

The chief executive officer of the United Church in B.C. was saying that I was fired and should be delisted because of my ideals! Imagine: sacked for not being able to "compromise"! Strike three, I thought, and they're out.

In any legitimate court of law, the judge probably would have dismissed the case against me at that point. But not in the church's cloud-cuckoo-land. The comedy had to play itself out, and end in complete farce, in the form of Benson's final witness.

I had never met Kathleen Hogman before, since she was the minister who was brought in especially by the church to replace me at St. Andrew's. Her sudden appointment was never voted on or discussed by the congregation, for she was a ringer, whose job it was to bury any remembrance of myself or my ministry in Port Alberni, while creating a "new face" for the church among the Alberni native bands, now that the residential school lawsuits had begun.

The only problem was, Hogman was slightly crazy.

She began her testimony by describing how she had hung a rope outside her office window at St. Andrew's church because of all the supposed "death threats" she was receiving.

"Death threats?" her lawyer asked.

"Yes, from all the people Kevin upset when he was ministering in town. I hung the rope out the window so I could make a quick escape if I had to."

Her comments continued in that kind of "sensible" vein.

"I go where the church sends me" she said during cross-examination. "I don't ask why, I just do my job. And I didn't need to ever meet Kevin to know what kind of a minister he was."

I couldn't imagine a clearer statement of hearsay, but it was allowed to stand as evidence. And it would have gone on like that, but for a major goof by Iain Benson.

The hearing had gone on for six months by then, instead of the couple of days of rapid rubber-stamping that the church had originally planned, and Benson was looking pretty worried. He had been paid over $50,000 by the church already, and he had not secured my expulsion. So he began to act desperate. He began soliciting evidence from people in the course of the hearing—something strictly forbidden by legal rules of procedure and ethics.

In this zeal, **Benson actually fabricated a letter from my church personnel committee that I had never seen before**, and which was clearly a fake because it had the wrong date on it, and referred to me as "Kevin Annett", my present name, when at the time my only name was "Kevin McNamee-Annett". But even this crude forgery was not the straw that broke the camel's back.

Benson procured a letter from Art Anderson, the official who had fired me, to "prove" that the church had had concerns about me for quite awhile. The letter was dated just a month after my firing, and, unfortunately for Benson, he didn't check its contents thoroughly before introducing it as evidence. **For the letter, which was written by Art Anderson, states that he was recommending that Presbytery break off all negotiations with me and deny me the chance to work elsewhere on the basis of the personal advice of Jon Jessiman.**

In short, the judge of the hearing had played a direct role in blocking a final resolution of my case, and had prevented me from earning a livelihood elsewhere.

Who could argue that Jessiman should not now step down as the hearing's judge?

My advocate, Bruce Gunn, moved that Jessiman be removed by the panel, based on the new evidence about his role in my case. The panel refused.

The farce had run its course, and I saw nothing beneficial anymore in contributing to it. Under legal advice, and weary of the charade, I left the hearing for good, explaining why in a written statement to the panel.

Of course, that didn't stop things—not in that Kafkaesque nuthouse. **The hearing continued, without the "defendant" present at all!** Now that I was gone, Benson introduced four letters critical of me to the panel—letters which had never been shown to myself or my advocate, and which he had in fact solicited that same week! Again, a completely illegal act. And again, perfectly acceptable to Miss Mollie and company.

The hangmen met for only another day, and then closed up shop. After all, the verdict had been decided before the hearing had ever begun.

In their final report, which was posted over the United Church internet, and still stands as the "official" church statement on my ministry and delisting, <u>none</u> of the thirty-eight letters of support for me which I submitted to the hearing panel are reprinted, or even referred to. But all four of Benson's illegally-obtained letters are quoted extensively by the Panel, for they were made-to-order "evidence" which "proved" my "unsuitability" as a minister.

In fact, the only thing that had been proved by the hearing was the disgusting depths to which top United Church officers will sink to cover up their history of foul deeds, and their silencing of critics within their own ranks.

The outcome was never in doubt. On March 7, 1997, I was expelled as a minister in the United Church, without any appeal allowed. The same day, I received a "Cease and Desist" letter from a G.R. Schmitt, a lawyer with Ferguson Gifford law firm in Vancouver, who, on behalf of the United Church, threatened to sue me if I spoke publicly about my delisting! Clearly, Big Jon and Lyin' Brian were worried that the farce would become known outside their incestuous little circle.

About ten people had thrown me out of the church, destroyed my public reputation, and denied my family and I a livelihood, without any delegated authority, ratification, or due process.

After my delisting, twenty four of the observers of this show trial wrote to Ujjal Dosanjh, the Attorney-General for BC, and demanded that he investigate the proceedings. Dosanjh, a cabinet colleague of John Cashore, refused, stating that the decisions of a church court were *"beyond the scope"* of his office—that is, the law.

It's official, then: the United Church of Canada is above the law of the land. (Some of these observers' letters are reprinted below).

Everything was arrayed against me during that silly charade of a hearing, but many new friends gathered around me in the course of those six months. One of them was Dr. Jennifer Wade, a founder of

Amnesty International in Vancouver who rallied the media to observe my "ludicrous show trial", as she described it, and who has since then proven to be a tireless advocate and defender of not only me but our campaign to expose genocide in Canada.

Another stalwart was my mother, Margaret Annett, who helped with my case and drew on her own personal knowledge of the church's railroading of me out of Port Alberni in her valiant efforts to appeal to the consciences of the delisting panel. Alas, such good seeds by mom fell on barren ground.

Finally, during most of the show trial, another friend, Alberni school survivor Harriett Nahanee, conducted a lonely vigil outside the west-end United Church in Vancouver where most of the hearing was held. In rain or shine, she paced the sidewalk, wearing a hand-made placard that read:

"504 years of Genocide: Where is Justice in the United Church?"

Harriett carried her message up and down the front of the church, talking to passersby, ignoring the hate stares from Jessiman and his cronies. For a few days, she was joined by Eugene, a native guy from Oyster Bay who helped her picket the church, and who told me of his own rape by priests at the Sechelt Catholic school when he was just nine years old.

I confess that I became so embroiled, at times, in the lies and stupidity going on in the hearing that I forgot all about Harriett. But when things got especially ridiculous, and one of my motions was once again ruled out of order by Jessiman, I would turn and see Harriett just outside the window, always there with her sign. And that was enough to keep me going.

One afternoon, I suddenly remembered who she reminded me of, and I went to tell her.

Soon after I began working at St. Andrew's, I looked out my office window one night and saw an old native man carrying a huge bag of something on his back. He stopped at the door to the church and tried to enter, but it was locked. He kept shaking the door handle, and finally shrugged and trudged off into the darkness, bearing his heavy load.

I never saw him again, and while I made sure to keep the church door unlocked as much as I could after that, I kept feeling the old man's burden on my own back. Until, one day, I found myself in the same place he was, on the other side of a locked church door. And then his load seemed to lighten a bit.

I told Harriett all of this, and she nodded knowingly. Oceans of culture and experience separated us, but I could see that she knew what I was thinking, and struggling with.

Although she learned many years ago to stifle her tears, and not let her rapists think they were crushing her, Harriett's sad brown eyes moistened as she said, "You might think they'll get away with this, Kevin, but they won't. I've had to wait fifty years for justice. Maybe you'll have to, too. But you can't ever give up. There are too many of us out here depending on you."

Her words were my transport out of the hell of my public defrocking, and my brutalising by the church, towards a new destiny—and a Tribunal.

....

Where there is official sanction for murder, there can be no regret, and no apology."

Simon Wiesenthal, Justice, Not Revenge

"It is absurd to talk of keeping faith with Indians."

General Phil Sheridan, 1878

By drawing so much attention to itself, and the scandals I surfaced, at the very moment that residential school victims were beginning to speak out and sue, the United Church committed a big mistake, compounding its problems enormously.

Instead of letting me wither and die in obscurity, or quiet me with another position in the church somewhere, United Church officials went out of their way to continue to give me public exposure by their unceasing attacks on me—and, by association, to the native survivors of their genocide, like Harriett Nahanee, who used my case to catapult their own stories into the limelight.

So determined were Jessiman and company to drive me from the church that they were unable to see the forest for the trees: to look beyond their own petty agenda of avenging themselves on me to the wider repercussions of publicly destroying the very minister who had blown the whistle on the church's crimes among west coast aboriginals.

And so all of the crap piled on me by these guys actually boomeranged against them, especially in the months after my formal "delisting". And that wasn't just because of the considerable media attention that was focused on my case.

By the spring of 1997, many people in the native community had come to identify with and trust me far more than they had while I was still in the church, <u>precisely</u> because of my mistreatment by church officials. And this trust by school survivors was critical to our launching of the first public Tribunal around the residential schools ever held in Canada, after the summer of 1997.

"You've got to be okay if the church is so pissed off at you" commented Dennis Tallio, an Alberni school survivor, to me when we first met at a Vancouver healing circle in September, 1997. "It means you did something right."

That was a typical sentiment among many of the survivors I met after my delisting, and it was an advantage I owe completely to the church's virulent campaign to expel and discredit me.

Like my own failed marriage, what seemed to me at first to be a defeat and a terrible loss turned out in fact to be a great gift, and an opportunity. But I only became aware of this advantage, and my renewed credibility, when Harriett Nahanee and others pointed it out to me, and encouraged me to join the residential schools healing circles as an advisor and a participant.

To be invited into such circles is a rare honour, accorded to few non-natives.

I had attended a few healing circles in Port Alberni, but they were tame affairs compared to what went on in the Vancouver native world.

Most Indians in Canada live off-reserve, where they struggle at a standard of living ranked sixty-fourth in the world, below that of

Thailand and Mexico. They are a literal third-world nation, poor and diseased, denied the benefits and bribes lavished on reserve and band-council natives by the federal government.

In effect, the off-reserve Indians are the descendents of the "expendable" children of the residential schools, and they are dying or being killed off at a rate ten times the national average. They are the living proof that the deliberate genocide of "unassimilable" Indians in Canada has never ended.

Many of these people congregate in Vancouver's downtown east side, among the cheap rooming houses and hotels of Hastings street. This skid-row became the soil out of which our movement began to grow.

They are a people completely neglected by their own leaders, and the "official" native organizations, which refused to take up the residential schools issue until pressure from below compelled them to do so. In fact, a huge vacuum of leadership exists in the urban native community because of the financial dependence of the Indian leaders on the very government that authorized the residential schools, and has so much to lose by an exposure of their real history.

Time and again, native leaders are forced by their position to engage in a continual balancing act between their own people and their federal government paymasters, whom they cannot risk alienating. As a result, these very leaders must ignore any issue which threatens to get "out of hand" in the eyes of Ottawa—like the residential schools furor.

The vacuum of leadership among aboriginals created by such a vacillating leadership allowed our meagre efforts to organize residential school survivors to pay off almost instantly, and provoke a dramatic response among ordinary natives who went through the schools.

After attending a number of healing circles, and hearing the same horror stories which were never finding their way into the media or public awareness, Harriett and I decided to form a group in July of 1997 which was committed not just to individual "healing" of the survivors but to raising the reality of genocide. We hoped to begin a movement that would result in the churches and the government being charged before the United Nations with crimes against humanity.

That struck a chord. When we held our first public forum in Vancouver, on February 9, 1998, an overflow crowd of five hundred, mostly native people turned out. This was the largest meeting around the residential schools ever held in Canada, and the title of the event—*"The Genocide Continues ... Murder, Corruption and Land Theft"*—set the tone that evening.

I hadn't appreciated the great chasm between the "official" native leadership and ordinary Indians until that forum. Speaker after speaker rose from the crowd to attack their leaders for doing nothing around the residential schools.

"They sit in their expensive offices all day and talk to white politicians, but they're never down here, where we are" yelled an elderly Shuswap man into the microphone, referring to the United Native Nations (UNN), the "official body" of urban natives in BC. "They don't know our pain. They're not poor like us. They're more white than the whites, just like the informers at residential school."

Five officials of the UNN were actually in attendance that night, and as each speaker slammed them, they shrank lower in their seats, and stared at the floor. None of them responded.

Another speaker, a young woman from the Native Youth Movement, leapt up and declared, "Why did it take a white minister here to bring out the truth about the murders in Port Alberni, when we all knew about them but were too afraid to speak?" she cried. "We've sat around for too long. It's time we occupied a few churches, and then the world will pay attention to us!".

That forum was really a turning point, initiating the first non-governmental Tribunal into residential schools later that year. But it also compelled the UNN and other "government Indian" organizations to finally climb on the bandwagon and go through the motions, at least, of demanding some justice for the survivors.

They were being pushed in that direction, reluctantly, by another force: the escalating numbers of lawsuits being launched by their own people against the churches and the federal government. During 1998, that number jumped from a few hundred to over 3,000 lawsuits across the country; by the spring of 2000 it was up to 8,000. There was big money to be made from the pain of the survivors, and not only the lawyers knew it.

Love and Death in the Valley

Suddenly, prominent native politicians became "outraged" over the residential school crimes, even though they had personally known of atrocities like the mass sterilisation of Indian women for many years, and had kept quiet. But, as with the RCMP or the churches, these Indian leaders spoke only of "physical and sexual abuse", <u>not</u> the deaths and torture of children. As if by some common agreement, which the media has faithfully adhered to, the deeper, documented crimes are rarely mentioned by the powers-that-be, whether "white" or "red".

This surprised me at first, but it is understandable, in the logic of lap-dogs. For native politicians, there is no money to be made by making an issue over genocide, when personal injury settlements hang like a juicy carrot in front of every Indian band across Canada. As well, some of the most prominent native leaders in BC are personally implicated in abuses and possibly the deaths of their fellow students while in the Alberni and Alert Bay schools, and these guys certainly have nothing to gain by opening the Pandora's Box of the atrocities more widely.

But in the end, it all comes down to who is paying the bills; and, raised as assimilated servants of a colonial Indian Affairs system, no "official" native leader will dare to really bite the hand that feeds them from Ottawa.

All of this has weighed against the state-funded native leadership supporting our efforts to bring the deeper truth of the residential schools to light, and public scrutiny. At this time, in 1998, even the more "militant" leaders of the UNN, like Viola Thomas, were mouthing the RCMP's line that "no children were deliberately killed in the residential schools", despite the growing evidence to the contrary.

By actually suppressing evidence of murders, which they have done time and again, native leaders have aided the efforts of church and state to obtain quick, out-of-court settlements with the survivors so that the facts, and perpetrators, of the deeper crimes will stay out of court, and the public record. Indeed, this has been the new strategy of the guilty parties in response to the growing threat that the full story of the residential schools will come out.

The state-funded native "leaders" have had an indispensable role to play in this latest cover-up, which utilises the legal system to bury evidence and silence witnesses to murder. Time and again, we have found that band council chiefs threaten their own people to keep silent about what they know of the deaths of children in the residential schools.

The churches, which were the most culpable actors in the daily atrocities, have the most to lose by this threatened exposure of murder, and so have generally kept out of sight as much as possible, relying on the government to take much of the heat around the residential schools. But this became harder for them to do when, in June of 1998, the first independent inquiry into the schools was opened in Vancouver under the sponsorship of a United Nations human rights agency.

Our Circle of Justice invited this agency, IHRAAM (The International Human Rights Association of American Minorities), to hold a Tribunal in the wake of our raucously successful public forum. IHRAAM responded by sending two of its officers, Rudy and Diana James, to interview some of our witnesses. The Jameses were "appalled" by what they heard, and quickly recommended that a Tribunal be held.

"This stuff is a matter for international law" Diana James told me, half-stunned, after she had spoken to a dozen of the survivors. "These are crimes against humanity, not 'personal injuries'. Why is no-one talking about that?"

Why, indeed? If I thought the United Church was a labyrinth of lies and fog, it was but a foretaste of the climate of denial and misinformation that has been built across Canada to hide the fact that a century of ethnic cleansing and mass murder is being swept under the rug.

We set out to try to reverse that through the IHRAAM Tribunal, where one revelation opened up another, more hideous one, implicating not only past criminals, but modern ones.

The Tribunal opened on June 12, 1998 to a crowd of over one hundred people at the Maritime Labour Centre in Vancouver's east end. A score of tribal judges from across the continent, along with U.N. observers, heard the testimony of several dozen survivors of west coast residential schools over a three day period. The testimonies were videotaped, and from the mountain of material from the UBC archives that I had accumulated, I provided corroborating documents to the Tribunal judges.

The witnesses to murder, sexual sterilisations, medical experiments and tortures were there that weekend in abundance, but the media were nowhere in sight. We had conducted a blitz of the national media, but no-one, save a solitary reporter from The Globe and Mail, attended the Tribunal.

Neither did any of the officials of church and state whom the Tribunal had subpoenaed, including Prime Minister Jean Chretien, the heads of Indian Affairs and the RCMP, and the leaders of the mainline churches. Some thirty four officials had been issued a "Diplomatic Summons" from the Tribunal to publicly answer charges of complicity in genocide. This Summons carried the weight of both the U.N. and international law behind it, but it was ignored, by all thirty four of them.

I consider that unfortunate, for the mandarins of power in Canada need to hear the voices of their victims. The latter were in abundance that weekend of the Tribunal. Many of them were near retirement, but their voices still broke with emotion as they recalled the tortures inflicted on them as children by the "official Christians".

"I don't know why those nuns hated me so much, when I was just a little kid" one of the women, from Vancouver Island, told the Tribunal judges. "But they held me down and shoved needles through my tongue when I was just eight years old. No-one would stop them; they could do whatever they wanted to us, and they did. They even killed young girls who got pregnant, and buried both mother and child in secret south of the Kuper Island school."

The water front union hall where we held the Tribunal was filled with a crowd of sobbing, struggling people that weekend. I imagined them as terrified children, hiding from rapists and sudden death, tortured and starved. And never had they spoken of their nightmare publicly until that moment. I discovered why quickly.

"We were forced to keep quiet" described an elderly man from Chemainus.

"First the priests and the Mounties, and then our own chiefs told us never to speak about our friends who were killed at the school. The priests invented fake stories of how the kids 'committed suicide'. It was a big conspiracy of silence, just like today."

As the weekend progressed, so did the courage of the witnesses who were there. By the second day, some of them began speaking about modern-day crimes, not only of past ones.

"I was told by my chief and council that I'd never get any funding for my college courses if I spoke at the Tribunal today" said a middle-aged Cowichan woman from southern Vancouver Island. "They've been threatening everyone on the reserve not to talk about what they know of the murders and the sterilisations."

When asked why native leaders would not want the full truth of the residential schools to be told, the woman replied, "It's because our chiefs are all child molesters themselves. They've been pedophiles ever since they were the enforcers for the priests at the Kuper Island school. They bugger our children all the time and Indian Affairs just looks the other way."

Her words encouraged others to come forward with even more disturbing tales. Two of them, Frank Martin and Helen Michel of the Carrier Nation of northern B.C., described their attempts to expose a native pedophile ring operating out of the Moricetown area.

"Our chief and council are shipping kids down to Vancouver and Seattle to a couple of safe-houses run by their friends" said Frank to the hushed gathering. "It's mostly young boys that are being sent. They end up at places like the Vancouver Club. The chiefs get a lot of money for pimping their own kids. There's judges and politicians involved, pretty senior ones. The whole thing has a lot of protection from the Mounties, 'cause every time we try to expose it we get arrested by them, or beaten up by the hired goons of the Carrier-Sekani chiefs."

His wife Helen described how her own nephew was abducted and "shared around" among wealthy pedophiles in Vancouver, and was then imprisoned on trumped-up charges for fourteen years to keep him quiet.

"These men will do anything to cover their sick acts" she said, as she struggled to speak amidst tears. "We've always been just cattle to them. Our own chiefs are striking deals with them to sell off our last natural resources. I've lost a lot of my family members who were murdered by chief and council to get their trap lines, so that they can be sold to The North American Water and Power Alliance, who want to divert all of our water and hydroelectricity down south."

Love and Death in the Valley

Helen also described her own tortures at a Catholic residential school near Kamloops, B.C. during the late 1960's, when she underwent a forced abortion after being raped by priests.

When the Tribunal judges concluded the hearing on June 14, 1998, they had documented forty-seven separate crimes against humanity committed in native residential schools in Canada between 1920 and 1984, including murder, rape, involuntary sterilisations, torture, medical experimentation and forced labour. All five of the definitions of Genocide in the U.N.'s International Convention on Genocide were found to have been perpetrated in the residential schools.

The main IHRAAM observer, Rudy James, told me that he had notified the U.N. Human Rights Commissioner in Geneva, Mary Robinson, that the Tribunal had found the government of Canada, the RCMP, and the Roman Catholic, United, Presbyterian and Anglican churches guilty in absentia of crimes against humanity.

The judges urged Ms. Robinson to launch a formal inquiry into the Canadian residential schools genocide, with the hope that she would lay charges against these guilty parties at the International Criminal Court. I personally sent over twenty hours of documented testimonies from that weekend to Ms. Robinson's office in Geneva.

Newsworthy stuff? Not in Canada, apparently. For not a single newspaper or media outlet, save one, ever reported the findings of the Tribunal, and none of its evidence or recommendations were ever acted upon by Mary Robinson's office.

However, the Tribunal did bring a storm of retaliation down on the heads of those witnesses who had summoned the courage to speak out. People who gave testimonies were beaten up, evicted from their homes on reserves, denied financial assistance and student loans from their band offices, and threatened with death if they ever again shared what they knew with investigators.

Even more serious repercussions fell on those who had pointed the finger at modern-day criminals. The two key witnesses to a native-run pedophile ring at the prestigious Vancouver Club involving politicians and judges, Frank Martin and Helen Michel of the Carrier Nation, were arrested without a warrant a few days after the Tribunal and held incommunicado for over a week, when they were both released without any charges been laid. Subsequently, they were physically attacked by a "band council goon squad", evicted from their home, denied welfare and re-arrested on trumped-up charges.

As well, Harriett Nahanee, who corroborated their account of the pedophile ring, had her home invaded and ransacked by an RCMP Tactical Squad on July 10, 1998, whose officers refused to show her any warrant.

During this same period, the brake lines to my car were cut, I received several death threats over the phone, and I was physically attacked on different occasions by the same two men in Vancouver's downtown east side.

"Some pretty senior people are worried about what you're uncovering about the kiddy sex ring" a source in the Union of BC Indian Chiefs told me just days after the Tribunal. "They say they're having you watched. Your name is on a list, so you'd better be careful, Kevin."

An even more interesting phone call came to me that month from Leo Knight, a former reporter with *The North Shore News* who is now a private security consultant.

"I investigated the Vancouver Club for two years, until I had to back off because I didn't want to get killed. There are definitely senior judges involved, and other powerful people. All I can say is that you're definitely on the right track."

To say that all of this began to spook me is to put it mildly. I had known for some time that the United Church's Alberni residential school, in particular, had been a source of native children for rich pedophiles for decades, and that church employees and ministers had made money off this child prostitution service. My getting close to this sordid fact while I was a minister in Port Alberni was one of the reasons that I had been fired and delisted so quickly. But this new evidence of a judicially-protected pedophile ring was even more dangerous, and harder to prove, since there are so few witnesses to it who are still alive.

A native lawyer named Renate Auger had tried to prove this in April of 1994, when she brought a lawsuit against two Supreme Court judges and the B.C. Law Society, charging them with protecting pedophiles and engaging in a criminal conspiracy. Renate was disbarred, her lawyer, Jack Cram, was dragged from court, drugged, and committed to Vancouver General's Psychiatric Hospital, and Renate was forced to flee the province under a death threat.

According to Elayne Crompton, a former law partner of Jack Cram's, the reason he was hammered so badly and silenced with drugs was because he had obtained photographic proof of sexual activity between young boys and the two senior judges in question, and he planned to use it in court.

The native connection here is that senior native politicians in B.C. are deeply engaged in the drug trafficking and child prostitution underworld, according to numerous witnesses, both native and white. They are allowed to do so by the government, in return for their cooperation during land claims and treaty negotiation talks, or over the residential schools litigation.

These chiefs are nearly all members of the "northern native group" of the United Church of Canada, the same group that paid off the Ahousaht band councillors to distance themselves from Chief Earl George and I over the Lot 363 deal. Indeed, four of these chiefs from Bella Bella were paid by the United Church to attend our Tribunal and intimidate witnesses into silence, according to one of them, Ed Martin of the Heiltsuk Nation.

I personally witnessesed them do so on the final day of the Tribunal, when one of them, Dean Wilson from Bella Bella, physically barred people from speaking at the microphone and even backed me into a corner and told me that I would "be in really deep shit" if I persisted with the Tribunal.

Such methods are known to many band members across BC. Only "white" people find it hard to believe.

Many of the members of the Circle of Justice group that helped organize the Tribunal were scared off or paid off after that weekend by these chiefs, and those connected with them, especially when the United Nations Human Rights Commission refused to act on our report. One by one people dropped away, or became unexplainably hostile, always with the same fear in their eyes.

Four of the members of the Circle of Justice, led by Amy Tallio, were even bribed by UNN officials and a police operative named James Craven to denounce me over the internet and urge native people to stay away from me and any future Tribunals. And the Tribunal's sponsor, IHRAAM, never took action with the UN Human

Rights Commission, apparently because of "strong pressure" applied to them by the Canadian government.

In fact, within a few months after the Tribunal, our entire investigation had been effectively shut down by an obvious sabotage campaign run by some force with a lot of money and professional expertise—in my opinion, probably the RCMP using native front men.

The Mounties, after all, have much to lose by our exposure of the residential schools holocaust, and the cover-up that has ensued.

The RCMP were the police arm of the residential schools and missionaries, being deputised under the Indian Act to take native children away from their parents and hunt down runaways from the schools. According to eyewitnesses like Harry Wilson of Bella Bella, RCMP officers concealed evidence of murdered children at the Alberni school, intimidated him and others into silence after they had discovered dead bodies, and then falsified death records to make murders look like "natural causes".

And yet, despite this, it is the Mounties who have been conducting the "official" investigation into the residential schools—kind of like delegating Richard Nixon to run the Watergate inquiry!

This typically farcical scenario—of the suspect in a crime controlling the process of investigating it—possibly explains why the RCMP have not exactly "gotten their man" during the six years of their supposed "hunt" for residential school criminals. In fact, at the time of this writing they've convicted just <u>two</u>.

From my experience, the Mounties have put far more time and energy into <u>preventing</u> an investigation into murders at the schools than in pursuing one. A key witness at our 1998 Tribunal confirmed this in her testimony on the first day.

This witness, whom I'll call "Charlene", is a native woman in her mid forties who worked as a counsellor in the government-funded "Residential School Project" in Chilliwack, BC, which was operated jointly with the RCMP.

"The whole so-called investigation by the Mounties into the residential schools is a joke" she told the Tribunal judges on June 12. "For over two years, we didn't investigate a single allegation of abuse or murder in a residential school. We had a budget close to one million dollars, but we mostly moved paper. We didn't offer a thing for victims. It was just a way to avoid doing anything.

"I can give you an example of this. Constable Gerry Peters of the RCMP Task Force flew into Bella Coola by helicopter in 1996 to meet with over 40 people who said they wanted to give their statements about the Alberni residential school. Peters arrived at noon but he took off almost immediately, without taking a single statement or talking to one of those people!

"It turned out that several of the local chiefs had been named by this group as child molesters themselves, so Peters backed right off, since they were chiefs on the government payroll who had pull in Ottawa. Peters was protecting those perverts."

This is not an isolated incident. The Mounties don't like taking testimonies of witnesses to murders in residential schools. They refused to accept Harriett Nahanee's written account of the murder of Maisie Shaw, or Archie Frank's—another eyewitness to a murder by Alfred Caldwell—or any of the statements arising from our Tribunal or numerous forums. In fact, on five different occasions since December, 1995, our investigators have offered affidavits to the RCMP from eyewitnesses which recount murder, torture and other atrocities at residential schools, and on <u>every</u> occasion they have been refused.

Precisely who the Mounties are protecting is not clear. But it is undeniable that they are impeding a real investigation into the residential schools and the deaths of native children; a fact epitomised by the aforementioned Constable Gerry Peter's statement to me, in October of 1997:

"We have never had a mandate to investigate homicide in those schools, and even if we had, it wouldn't happen."

As to the RCMP's role in actually subverting our Tribunal, it was Gerry Peter's predecessor, Sgt. Paul Willms, who threatened me in June of 1996 in the parking lot of CKNW radio in downtown Vancouver, after we had appeared together on an open-line program. Our conversation is informative of the regime of cover-up and intimidation that surrounds the residential schools:

Paul Willms (PW): Before you go, I'd like to ask you to clear things with us before you send out any more of your press releases about dead children.

Kevin Annett (KA): Pardon me?

PW: It's just that things are getting out of hand, with you and Mrs. Nahanee making all those wild accusations about murders. Things are going too far, and some people may do something to stop it.

KA: What people? Is that a threat?

PW: No, just a warning. I think for your own safety you should check with me before doing any more press releases.

KA: I thought we lived in a democracy. So why should we come to you guys?

PW (exasperated): Look, Nahanee's not a credible witness. Even if Caldwell was still alive, he'd never be convicted in this province.

KA: Oh really? I thought you were supposed to be an investigator. Isn't that your job, to investigate, and not be the judge and jury, too?

PW: You heard what I said. Some people are getting upset over what you're alleging, and they may stop you.

KA: This is ridiculous. (walks away).

Sometimes the machine is subtle, and sometimes it's not. But its objective remains the same: to keep corpses buried, truth fogged, and land, money and power in the same old hands.

Small forces of life are pushing against all that, like gentle slivers of grass breaking through sidewalk concrete. It's a labour of unexplainable love and pain to nurture those slivers while your life is threatened, and in tatters, and all you want to do is strike back and wipe away all the lies and filth, but you can't.

A group of seven very brave men and women helped to do so during our Tribunal; people near the end of their lives, but with a story that needs to be nailed on the door of every church and government office in Canada.

These eyewitnesses were kidnapped and hauled off to the Catholic Kuper Island school when they were very young, and between them they experienced every one of the five crimes defined by the U.N. Convention on Genocide, which the Canadian government ratified in 1952.

They were sexually sterilised, and beaten, and taken against their will into captivity. They were sodomised, and saw their little friends murdered. And they were used in undisclosed drug-testing experiments in the winter of 1939 by "German speaking doctors" and priests, under the supervision of the RCMP and government Indian Agents.

When these survivors went to the Catholic church for recognition in the 1960's, they were threatened by Victoria Bishop Remi de Roo, who told them they would "be arrested" if they told their story to anyone.

When they asked the RCMP to exhume the graves of their murdered friends on Kuper Island, they were refused, and threatened that if they told of what they knew they would be imprisoned or even killed.

Finally, they came to our Tribunal to find, if not justice, at least a forum in which to speak the unspeakable.

Arnold Sylvester, one of these survivors, spoke to me in his home near Duncan, on Vancouver Island, after the Tribunal, in August of 1998. His words reminded me again of the price of allowing the voiceless to talk, and of the cold comfort that having done so brings people like he and I when the big boot crushes us in response.

"Those doctors used us like lab rats to try out their drugs. We were nothing to them. Two of my best friends died after getting those shots. They were only ten years old. But the doctors did it with such calmness in their eyes, like they knew they were safe and would get away with it.

"We knew they'd get away with it, because they had the government and the churches behind them. You feel small and powerless up against people like that, because you know that once you take them on, you're finished for good. That's why we've been afraid to talk for so many years.

"But I still have to know why they did it. I may have been scared, but those men were more scared, because they knew they were guilty, even if they had the power on their side. I still am trying to find out why they did it to us, why they were trying to wipe us all out like that. And as long as I keep asking why, they're going to be scared of me.

"I guess you could say the residential schools were a big success. They were put there to destroy us. They called us devil worshippers, you know, but it was the whites who worshipped evil, and killed innocent children. Maybe none of this will make any difference, but at least I know the truth, and now you do, too."

....

Love and Death in the Valley

-22-96 MON 11:28 VALERIE CAIRNS

THIS IS EXHIBIT H
REFERRED TO IN THE AFFIDAVIT
OF ...PATRICIA GUBERT...
SWORN BEFORE ME THIS 23
DAY OF ...JAN... 19 96

JANUARY 22, 1996

ATTENTION: MS. MARNIE DUNNAWAY, FAX# 1-604-681-8339

RE: MINISTERIAL PERFORMANCE OF THE REVENEND KEVIN ANNETT

DEAR MADAM;

Over the past four years I have shared and witnessed a good deal of the public ministry of the Reverend Kevin Annett. I have also shared in personal discussions on the nature of his difficulties with his congregation and United Church officials on the Island, as he likewise shared in my own.

In every way I consider his work to have been exemplary. His conduct of public worship was thoughtful, insightful, and impactful on a growing number of Port Alberni residents. On two separate occasions I personally witnessed his conduct of public worship: once unobserved by Kevin, and once seated with his congregation. On both occasions, in spite of the difficulties he was facing, I found Kevin's words and actions to be honest and forthright yet open and conciliatory. Those services of worship were a tribute to "Good Order" in the best of Presbyterian tradition.

Kevin's community ministry was dynamic and heartfelt. Several times I have met with community groups with which he was associated and appreciated the incisive leadership he provided. On one occasion we tracked down the survivors of a tenement fire and I experienced Kevin visibly shaken at the news of a resident's death, and focused on assisting with the necessary follow-up. Community ministry was/is his forte.

And, having said that, I want also to add that Kevin's work with the disadvantaged was guided by an intellect honed by his knowledge of the leading Biblical scholars and theological writers of our times. Kevin's ministry was not in any way a mindless "do good-ism". His sermons were a testament to that: and I know because I often stopped on my way through "Port" to the West Coast and picked up a copy of his latest sermon from a rack inside the Church entrance. They were worth reading and prompted more than one good thought for my own ministry.

All of this is to testify that Kevin is just one of many current day clergy, well-trained and astute to the realities of a changing world, who find themselves in institutional hierarchies captivated by "out-moded thinking" minorities in the cultural back-waters of the Church. What happened to Kevin in Port Alberni was predictable if your add to the above qualities what the Executive Secretary of the United Church Conference Office said: "Kevin's problem, if he has one, is that he is unwilling to compromise, unlike most of the rest of us who have managed to survive (in this institution)." To illustrate the point in the context of the Port Alberni culture--the Anglican Church there last week, led by a white South African born minister voted to "disaffiliate" from the Anglican Church of Canada over the National Churches' stance on human sexuality and the authority of the

Kevin Annett

Scriptures. Communities like Port Alberni provide the cultural backdrop in our society against which the term "politically correct" derives its meaning.

I would hope that this little aside will help you and the others facing this most unfortunate situation of Kevin and Anne's marriage breakdown to understand the enormous pressures they have been under, and against which few marriages would survive. I trust it will also shed some light on the quality of Kevin's ministry in Port Alberni and the inherent difficulties he encountered.

SWORN BEFORE ME at the City of)
Victoria, at the Province of British)
Columbia the 22nd day of January, 1996.)
)
_____   )   _____
A Commissioner for taking Affidavits)   Reverend Bruce W. M. Gunn
in the Province of British Columbia)
VALERIE M. CAIRNS
NOTARY PUBLIC
106-4475 VIEWMONT AVE.
VICTORIA, B.C. V8Z 6L8
479-5001

NO ADVICE REQUESTED NOR GIVEN.
ATTESTED ONLY BUT NOT DRAWN.

Love and Death in the Valley

Cecilia's Tomb: The slum apartment in Port Alberni
gutted by fire on September 5, 1995, claiming the life
of Ahousaht woman, Cecilia Joseph

Naming the Criminal: The Public Testimonies of Two Witnesses to the Murder of Native Children by Rev. Alfred Caldwell, The Vancouver Sun, 18 and 20 December, 1995

The Vancouver Sun, MONDAY, DECEMBER 18, 1995

Claim of murder goes back to '40s

KAREN GRAM
Vancouver Sun

RCMP are launching an investigation today into an allegation that a young girl was murdered at a United Church residential school for Indians on Vancouver Island 50 years ago.

Art Anderson, an official with the United Church, said Sunday that police were notified of the allegation as soon as the church learned of it.

Rev. Kevin McNamee-Annett, a former United Church minister for the Alberni area, reported the allegation to the current minister Thursday. On Friday, both McNamee-Annett and the church lawyer reported it to the police.

"We are uncertain what this means, but we have to treat it seriously," Anderson said. "As of tomorrow, the police will be beginning an investigation.

The investigation was triggered by a statement from a North Vancouver woman who told McNamee-Annett she was nearby when a six-year-old girl was kicked down some stairs and died.

Harriet Nahanee, 60, is the first witness to come forward to support recent allegations about killings at residential schools on the island.

DEADLY NIGHTMARES: Harriet Nahanee, 60, says she is haunted by a murder she witnessed at a United Church residential school in Port Alberni 50 years ago.

In another case, a boy is said to have bled to death after he was beaten as punishment for breaking a jar at the school in Ahousaht in the 1940s.

Reports of sexual and physical assaults at the Port Alberni area school sparked a province-wide investigation of residential schools by an RCMP task force. It has been gathering evidence for about one year.

Please see RCMP, B3

RCMP: Memory sparks tears

Continued from page 1

In interview with The Vancouver Sun, Nahanee said she can't remember the girl's name but she knows that she came from Nitinat Lake and her father's name was Blackie.

"I remember her from Nitinat Lake," she said. "Every so often her name comes to me and I can see her face."

Nahanee said the girl died in 1946, when Nahanee was 11 years old. But the memory is still painful enough that she cried throughout the telling.

"I was at the bottom of the stairs in the basement," she said. "I always went to the bottom of the stairs to sit and cry.

"I heard her crying, she was looking for her mother. I heard [the school administrator] yelling at the supervisor for letting the child run around on the stairwell.

"I heard him kick her and she fell down the stairs. I went to look — her eyes were open, she wasn't moving. They didn't even come down the stairs. They were arguing at the top of the stairs.

"I never saw her again."

Nahanee said other students later told her the girl had died and her body had been sent back to Nitinat Lake.

Nahanee told the other children what she had heard. She told her mother and many of the elders in her tribe, but nobody believed her, the woman said. She body believed her, the woman said. She didn't trust the RCMP so she didn't report it to them.

Rev. A.E. Caldwell, a United Church minister, was head of the school for four years Nahanee lived there. She said lepers he regularly sexually assaulted her in the infirmary.

- In a written statement which has been forwarded to the RCMP task force, Nahanee says she was taken, every week to the infirmary where either Caldwell or the boys' supervisor, a Mr. Peake, would force her to perform oral sex.

Nahanee said she believes other deaths, which at the time the church said were the result of exposure when students tried to run away, were really caused by beatings in the school barn.

"The woman still has nightmares about the killing and lives with rage and shame resulting from her treatment.

"I would love to be free of the shame — to leave all that behind me and have some pride in myself."

Love and Death in the Valley

Vancouver Sun, December 20, 1995

Beaten to death for theft of a prune

Indian elder recalls strapping of 15-year-old boy at Island residential school in 1938 by United Church minister.

MARK HUME
Vancouver Sun

A 15-year-old boy who stole a prune from a jar in the kitchen of a United Church residential school was strapped so relentlessly his kidneys failed him and he later died in bed, says a native Indian elder who was there at the time.

Archie Frank, now 68, was just 11 years old when his school mate, Albert Gray, was caught stealing in the Ahousat Residential School kitchen one night in 1938.

Frank, a retired commercial fisher, says he's never forgotten what happened to Gray, a husky youngster from the remote Vancouver Island community of Nitinat.

"He got strapped to death," said Frank in an interview on Tuesday.

"Just for stealing one prune, [Rev. A.E.] Caldwell strapped him to death. Beat the s— right out of him."

Frank's story, told after a 57-year silence, crystallizes much of what the furore over residential schools is all about.

For the past year the RCMP has been probing a series of alleged abuses at church-run residential schools. So far they have found evidence that 54 people were victims of abuse at the hands of 94 offenders. The investigation is concerned with 14 residential schools operated by the Anglican, United and Roman Catholic churches from the late 1800s to 1984.

The First United Church has come under scrutiny by the RCMP this week because of new allegations that two children were killed while at the residential school in the Port Alberni area in the 1940s and '50s.

Frank said Caldwell left Ahousat after the residential school burned down in 1940 and went on to be principal of the United Church school in Port Alberni.

Please see SCHOOL, A2

SCHOOL: Beaten to death for theft of a prune

Continued from page 1

Frank said Gray was caught with his hand in the prune jar by the night watchman at the Ahousat school.

"The day after he got strapped so badly he couldn't get out of bed. The strap wore through a half inch of his skin.

"His kidneys gave out. He couldn't hold his water anymore," said Frank, who has never told his story to the police.

He said Gray lay in his bed for several weeks after the beating, while he and another boy at the school cared for him, bringing him meals, and changing the urine-soaked sheets on his bed.

"They wouldn't bring him to a doctor. I don't think they wanted to reveal the extent of his injuries," said Frank, who still lives in the tiny village of Ahousat, just outside Tofino on the west coast of Vancouver Island.

Frank said he spent several years attending the First United Church residential school in Ahousat, and for the most part found it to be a good place.

"I had a very good experience in that school.

"That was the only one [bad incident] I experienced," said Frank of the death of his friend.

He said he never thought of reporting the death at the time because he was only 11 years old and because the principal of the school was seen as the ultimate authority.

When he grew older he sometimes remembered Gray, he said, but didn't go to the police because his philosophy was: "Keep out of harm's way — and learn to forgive."

Frank was asked why he thought a boy would be beaten so severely for such a minor offence.

"I don't know how you guys operate. That's not the Indian way," he replied.

Frank said he's aware of a province-wide inquiry into residential schools by the RCMP, but it's not something he wants to get caught up in.

"I don't want to get involved for something that happened so long ago,"

Frank also said there seems little point because Caldwell is now dead.

"There's no use having hard feelings for a dead man. If he was alive, I'd still be angry," he said.

Rev. Bruce Gunn, the United Church minister in Ahousat, said Frank's attitude of forgiveness is typical of the older generation of Indian people.

"Their tradition was to get along because they lived in survival cultures. They knew how important it was to forgive," he said.

But Gunn said younger Indian people feel it's important to get to the bottom of what happened, and they are pressing for inquiries into crimes that may have happened more than 50 years ago.

Gunn said he has been talking to elders in Ahousat, trying to confirm some of the stories that have been going around.

He hadn't talked to Frank, but said he would.

Attention was drawn to the United Church residential school system on Vancouver Island earlier this month when Jack McDonald, a candidate for the New Democratic Party leadership, called for a public inquiry into alleged deaths at schools in the Port Alberni area.

McDonald said he'd heard of at least two deaths, one of which was in Ahousat.

Sgt. Paul Willms, who is heading the RCMP investigation into abuse at B.C. residential schools, said he hadn't heard any allegations about deaths in the Port Alberni area until McDonald brought them up.

The police in Port Alberni this week began questioning witnesses and promised a thorough investigation.

Meanwhile, Kevin McNamee-Annett, a former United Church minister, issued a statement Monday saying he's going on a fast to protest against the church's handling of the issue.

McNamee-Annett was fired by the Port Alberni presbytery last January. He claims he was dismissed for trying to unearth the truth about the residential schools.

But United Church representative Rev. Art Anderson said McNamee-Annett was let go because he wasn't doing a good job.

McNamee-Annett said that by undertaking his fast he hopes "to bring greater public and moral attention to the wrongs and negligence at work within the United Church. In this way, the community as a whole can call the church back to its true spirit: that of truthful, just and loving people who the servants of the poor."

Kevin Annett

Church-school victim got no help

The Province, Tuesday, October 27, 1998, A13

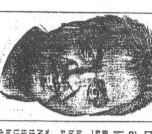

MARLON WATTS mourns brother

Native man's death blamed on stress of abuse by 'monster,' lengthy legal battle

By Suzanne Fournier
Staff Reporter

Marlon Watts wants to know how many more men will die before victims of residential-school sexual abuse see justice.

Marlon's brother Darryl, whose body was found drifting in Nanaimo harbour Saturday, was the second death among 30 plaintiffs who are suing Ottawa and the United Church for abuse they suffered at the Alberni Indian Residential School.

Darryl Watts, who was depressed and drinking, left court Thursday morning despondent that the United Church had demanded the victims' civil suit be postponed until April.

He never returned to hear the end of the day for a settlement conference, something the church has adamantly refused in the past.

"I'll never see my brother again, because he never got the help he needed to help him cope with the trauma of being raped when he was four, by a monster the church had just retired," said Marlon Watts, a 42-year-old Vancouver-based counsellor for the Native Courtworkers.

"There were no healing funds for my brother, no matter how many times we applied. No one had money or time for him, not the United Church or the federal government who employed the pedophile who abused Darryl, not the $350-million so-called federal healing fund.

"If any of that money had been made available, my brother would still be alive."

A coroner has ruled the death an accident, but Watts called it "accidental suicide."

Another plaintiff, Simon Danes, committed suicide before the Alberni case came to court.

Now the family wants the church or government to pay for Darryl Watts' body to be returned to the Nisga'a village of Laxgalts'ap, said Marlon, "so we can give Darryl a proper burial."

The plaintiffs' lawyer, Allan Early, said the United Church finally agreed Thursday to settlement talks, after new evidence was introduced from the church's own archives. Documents show that in 1960, the church and Ottawa were informed of widespread sexual abuse at the schools but responded with a directive to keep the incidents out of the media.

Arthur Plint was rehired by the school in 1963 and within a year had sexually abused all four Watts brothers.

Between 1948 and 1968, Plint is believed to have molested hundreds of native boys.

The boys' mother, Marie Watts, testified that neither she nor her husband, who was illiterate, signed documents produced by the church that surrendered her boys to school.

Marlon noted that when Darryl took the stand last February, he was "raked over the coals" by church lawyer Christopher Hinkson, who accused him of "recovered-memory syndrome."

Admission of the Cover-up by church and state of Crimes at the Alberni Residential School, The Province, 27 October, 1998

Love and Death in the Valley

Letters of Witnesses to the Delisting 'Kangaroo Court' that expelled Kevin Annett from United Church ministry, 1997

JACK BELL, B.A.Sc., LL.D, O.B.C., C.M.
Suite 2703 - 2055 Pendrell Street
Vancouver, B.C. V6G 1T9

Telephone (604) 683 - 7835
Fax (604) 669 - 1861

June 20, 1997

Jennifer Wade
6061 Highbury Street
Vancouver, BC V6N 1Z2

Dear Jennifer:

I attended to the "Trial" of Reverend Annett a short while ago and was absolutely disgusted in the way it was handled.

While I have never been to a "kangaroo court" I have read about them and this certainly had all the earmarks of one.

This man who tried to do good apparently stepped on some big toes and they tried to get rid of him.

Certainly a mockery of justice and a disgrace for the United Church.

Yours truly;

Jack Bell

Jack Bell

Kevin Annett

Glenda Leznoff
2231 Waterloo St.
Vancouver B.C.
V6R 3H2

July 10, 1997

To Whom it May Concern,

Last fall I sat in on a session of the United Church's delisting hearing of Kevin Annett. I am neither a friend of Mr. Annett nor a member of the United Church. I came as a curious spectator having heard several conflicting reports about the situation of Mr. Annett.

As the session proceeded I became more and more uncomfortable and offended by both the method and mood of this hearing. Clearly, Mr. Annett was being prosecuted, tried and judged by officials of the United Church in the kind of trial that makes mockery of any democratic legal system. This is the kind of trial that Arthur Koestler wrote novels about and that Robert Bolt wrote a play about -- the kind of trial where the trappings of legality are used to give the "courtroom" a semblance of authority and due process. But how could there be due process when the judges had hired the prosecutor, when the judges and prosecutor followed legal rules only when it pleased them, and when the accused was not informed about the shifting charges and procedures?

I think it both dangerous and deceitful to have lawyers mixed up in affairs such as this one. Surely, it is the responsibility of the courts of Canada and British Columbia to make sure that its members show proper respect for the laws of this land by acting as befits their status as legal representatives, not pawns for some religious show trial.

I am sorry to say that I cannot comment on the details of the case in its entirety. After one session, it was clear to see that Mr. Annett had been tried and convicted by the United Church before this so-called trial ever began.

Sincerely,

Glenda Leznoff

Glenda Leznoff

Description of the Hearing to Delist Rev. Kevin Annett

by Dr. Jennifer Wade

One would have to have attended the sessions held by the United Church of Canada here in Vancouver to believe to what extent a church will go to silence and punish one of its own.

When I first read Stephen Hume's story in The Vancouver Sun about Rev Annett being fired from his church in Port Alberni for having criticized the church for its profitable sale of native land and for having invited the natives to speak from his pulpit (Sun , July 10, 1995), I felt something had to be very wrong.

To be threatened with a delisting surely this man had to be guilty of something absolutely awful . But no. Church officials made it clear right off that he had done nothing wrong and there were no charges against him.. In that vein, an Alice-in Wonderland type of hearing began with the senior official for the Church Conference Office in B.C., Rev. Brian Thorpe, setting up the hearing , choosing the three panel members, and himself giving testimony against Rev. Annett. Prior to this, it came out in testimony that he had discussed Rev. Annett's case with a journalist.

At this hearing, the Church itself has been represented by two salaried lawyers and salaried ministers. Annett, who has been unemployed for over two years now, had only his mother as advocate at the beginning of the hearing until a fellow minister, Rev. Bruce Gunn, who knows Annett's work well and has described it as "exemplary," volunteered to take over ---- a very brave action indeed, considering the moveable goalposts and arbitrary rulings of this hearing .

As an observer, I have attended every day of this hearing but one ---- that is until Rev. Annett had to withdraw because of the mounting absurdities and his very real need to keep a roof over his head. Out of the four people who testified against him, not one had heard him preach nor seen him in action among his parishioners. One of the four people had never even met him until she came to give testimony, and there was talk of putting her testimony in camera undoubtedly to keep out press and observers. Of the three others testifying against Annett, one admitted to having had very little face-to-face contact, the other admitted twenty nine times in two and a half hours " I do not know," " I was not there," " I cannot speak to that," and Rev. Brian Thorpe himself had only met with Annett to discuss difficulties in a Horseshoe Bay restaurant for less than an hour.

At the outset of the hearing, it was announced that the criteria for judging Rev. Annett would only be established after the hearing was completed. This has allowed the criteria for deciding Annett's fitness for ministry to change day by day. A further absurdity is that supposed letters of complaint that were the basis for Annett's removal from his pulpit do not in fact appear to exist. And the most recent absurdity is that the United Church lawyers have told Rev. Annett that conceivably he might have to pay the costs of

Kevin Annett

the hearing. Was Joan of Arc ever asked to pay for the wood that burned her?

There have been other ministers threatened with de-listing who backed off from taking a stand, but Rev. Annett did not. He stood his ground and fought back without a lawyer, without any money, without a job, and without friends in higher church circles. Nor did Rev. Annett escape the time-worn criticism of all dissidents, known to Amnesty International, that something was "psychologically" wrong. What has amazed observers is the punishment he has taken from the church for two years, and yet giving his testimony, he has remained calm, reasonable, extremely truthful and convinced of his rightness.

During the questionable proceedings of this hearing, complaints to the B.C. Law Society have been submitted about both church lawyers for unprofessional conduct, for prejudicial bias, and for conflict of interest. This has not been the finest hour for the United Church. Little wonder that its adherents are decreasing, while expensive lawsuits against it are increasing. It is surprising how few United Church members have questioned that well over $300,000 of their contributions have been spent to delist this man when he could not get the same church to continue operating a food bank in Port Alberni for $1,000 a month. Indeed, he was issued an ultimatum by the church to close this food bank.

It is interesting that Rev. Annett was removed from his pulpit and threatened with de-listing only two months after he had criticized the church's controversial "land-grab" in Ahousaht. The church declares that Annett is being removed for his "manner". One cannot help but remember that Thomas More, many centuries ago, was told that he was to be beheaded for his "behaviour." Little wonder that Rev. Annett's many attempts to reconcile with the church have been thwarted, since it would appear that the clear aim of church officials from the beginning has been to get him out of the church.

Without any charges against him, the de-listing hearing cannot be anything but bizarre and cruel. What better example of this could there be than the written threat read by the Panel's chairperson as Rev. Annett and his advocate withdrew, that they would now face "dire consequences".

On March 7th a Vancouver law firm wrote Rev. Annett--- and his mother!---that they must cease and desist from any further criticism of the United Church or its offficials.

Dr. Jennifer A. Wade
6061 Highbury Street
Vancouver, BC
V6N 1Z2
604-263-4727

Love and Death in the Valley

Dr. M.K.Gottle
3951, West 20th Avenue
Vancouver, B.C.
V6S 1G3
June 30, 1997

Re: Hearing by The United Church, B.C.Conference
concerning de-listing of Rev. Annett

My general impression of this hearing is that it will remain a very black mark against the United Church of Canada. It was a most shameful way to treat a member of the church ministry and I have no doubt that it could be shown to be unlawful in its constitution and procedure. This hearing appeared to be a 'witch hunt' perpetrated by the hierarchy of the church whose previous action (in the sale of land) had been questioned by Rev. Annett. The church was apparently humiliated (embarassed by the truth being known) and it appears the directive was that Rev.Annett must be dismissed by whatever means necessary without regard to costs. If I had not attended some of the sessions I would not have believed that the church would act in this way. It was a most disquieting procedure and painful for an observer to realize what was being done and who was ulitimately responsible for it. One disturbing aspect of the hearing was the condescending attitude displayed by the Judicial Officer and the panel members toward Rev. Annett and his advocate. Ironically, the hearing was preceded by a prayer imploring 'God' through his 'son' to aid them in their task. What little regard and respect for spiritual leadership to be addressed before such a sham.

Some specific questions are:

1. What was Rev. Annett's crime? Nothing was ever stated. Was he too truthful and conscientious for the church?

2. Why was this hearing complete with paid lawyer, panel and court reporter allowed? Surely a consensual type of procedure to resolve the problems (as attempted by Rev. Annett on numerous occasions; see his statement of Mar. 3, 1997) would have been a more credible procedure for a Christian group?

3. Why was Mr. Jon Jessiman made the Chief Judicial Officer of the hearing when he was known to have acted for B.C.Conference and Comox-Nanaimo Presbytery in many aspects of Rev. Annett's dismissal, (see motion to B.C. Conference De-listing Panel by Rev. B. Gunn, Feb 19,1997)?

4. Why did the church not make use of Rev. Annett's skill and experience in working with the underprivileged to attempt to address some of the social problems about which the church is theoretically very concerned?

-2-

5. Is the general membership of the United Church of Canada aware of this waste of funds (lawyer's fees, court reporter panel members and facilities) for holding such a 'witch hunt'? I am certain that should members realize that their contributions were used in this way there would be cries of outrage. In addition to the waste of funds the wasting the time of personnel who, one would expect, would have more important work and activities in which to be involved is surely a concern.

6. If such a procedure can occur under the supposedly good offices of the United Church of Canada what other groups or institution may be allowed to operate in this way?

Signed,

Dr. M.K. Cottle

Love and Death in the Valley

No Longer Hidden: Poster for the first public forum into the deaths of children at Indian residential schools, Vancouver, 9 February, 1998

Kevin Annett

War Crimes Tribunal: Public Invitation and Summons of IHRAAM, sponsoring agency of first Tribunal into crimes in Canadian residential schools, and the sole media coverage of this Tribunal

INTERNATIONAL HUMAN RIGHTS ASSOCIATION OF AMERICAN MINORITIES | IHRAAM |

An International NGO in Consultative Status (Roster) with the Economic and Social Council of the United Nations

You are invited to add your testimony about native residential schools to the voice of many, at an International Human Rights Tribunal, June 12-14, 1998, in Vancouver, B.C.

The *International Human Rights Association of American Minorities* (IHRAAM), an affiliate of the United Nations with consultative status, is conducting an inquiry into allegations of murder and other atrocities at native residential schools in British Columbia. This inquiry will include a panel of international human rights experts, who will receive testimony and examine all evidence.

The panel will come to a verdict about the guilt or innocence of church, government and police officials in the reported deaths and torture of native children at the residential schools. Their findings and verdict will be forwarded to the Secretary-General of the United Nations, the Human Rights Commission and to the international media.

If you have personal, family or any kind of knowledge of the abuse, torture and murder of native people at the residential schools and the inter-generational legacy of the residential school system, please attend this tribunal so that the full truth of the schools can be made known and healing can begin. Testimonies can be made either in full confidence at the public tribunal or in private.

The Tribunal will be held at the Maritime Labour Centre, 1880 Triumph St., in Vancouver, commencing at 9:00 a.m. each day. For more information, contact the *International Human Rights Association of American Minorities*, c/o Rudy James, at 425-483-9251 or, in Vancouver, contact The Circle of Justice c/o Kevin at 462-1086 or Harriett at 985-5817.

Thlau Goo Yailth Thlee, The First and Oldest Raven
Rudy James
Member, Board of Directors   Dated this *16th day of April 1998*

Love and Death in the Valley

NORTHWEST INTERNATIONAL-TRIBUNAL COURT
International Tribunal of Original Nations and Invited Tribunal Jurists
Indigenous Holders of Allodial Title

A Convening of the Original Hereditary Forum of Justice

DIPLOMATIC DISPATCH & SUMMONS

To: Mr. Brian Thorpe, Executive Secretary United Church of Canada, B.C.

Please be advised that you have been listed as a primary witness in an adjudication of a matter before this Court, which is a Tribunal of International and Indigenous Judges. Therefore, your presence is Hereby respectfully requested:

On June 12-14, 1998 at 9:00 AM
At the Maritime Labour Centre
1880 Triumph St., Vancouver, BC

Said Tribunal is convening pursuant to traditional tribal law, the Rule of Natural Law, and the Law of Nations and your attendance is requested to participate in the examination of issues and questions regarding this matter.

Cause No. NWITC-0612-98CCAN

The charges are titled: Forced Removal from Traditional Lands and Waters, Institutional Racism, Physical and Psychological Warfare, Genocide, and Murder, stemming from the Residential School System supported by the Government of Canada and the United Church of Canada, the Catholic Church and other Churches, Organizations and Individuals involved with the operation of Residential Schools across Canada and the Northwest Territories.

You may desire to consult with your attorney in regards to this matter, or have an advocate of your choice attend the hearings with you. You may submit written documents and materials, but be advised that they do not carry the same weight as personal testimony.

Due to the Nation Status of the Original Nations of the North and South American Continents and Hawaii (the Holders of allodial Title) this is a Nation to Nation issue, thereby mandating the presence of representatives from the Government of Canada. Internationally known Human Rights experts from the International Human rights Association of American Minorities, a United Nations NGO with consultative status, will observe the proceedings. Reports will be submitted to the High Commissioner of the Human Rights Commission.

Filed and Noted:
May 23, 1998
HyrielGay
Administrator for the NWITC

Signed this 22nd day of May, 1998
Lead Judge WhatStaw, George Suckinaw James, Jr.

DIPLOMATIC DISPATCH & INVITATION TO TESTIFY
NorthWest International Tribunal • PO Box 1546 • Woodinville, WA 98072
Ph/Fax: 425-483-9251 or 206-362-7725 • Email: wolfhouse48@hotmail.com

Kevin Annett

Probe of Canadian residential schools to be reported at UN

Globe & Mail, June 20, 1998

BY ROBERT MATAS
British Columbia Bureau

VANCOUVER — An international human-rights group investigating allegations of racism at Canada's residential schools for native children expects to deliver its report next month to United Nations Human Rights Commissioner Mary Robinson.

Representatives from the International Human Rights Association of American Minorities were in Vancouver earlier this month to hear from several natives who had been placed in residential schools. The association is formally affiliated with the United Nations.

Charlene Strong Eagle, a member of the tribunal hearing the allegations, criticized the federal government and the United, Anglican and Roman Catholic churches yesterday for not appearing at the tribunal to respond.

Those who spoke during a three-day forum recounted their experiences at the schools and some stated they had witnessed what they described as murder, rape, sexual molestation, routine beatings and electric shock to five-year-old children who misbehaved.

They also said that young native women were involuntarily sterilized, that abortions were induced in pregnant students and that native children were kidnapped and placed forcibly in the residential schools.

Accounts of the offences were given by 27 former students at eight residential schools in B.C., according to a list distributed yesterday by Kevin Annett, a former United Church minister who has done extensive research on the alleged abuses.

A report accompanied by 19 hours of videotaped testimony from former students will be presented to Ms. Robinson on July 31 in London, England, Mr. Annett said in an interview. The human-rights group will ask Ms. Robinson to have the report presented to a UN Human Rights Commission meeting in New York in August, he added.

The human-rights group is also planning to ask the World Council of Churches this summer to start an inquiry into the role of the Anglican and United churches in Canada's residential schools for natives, Mr. Annett said.

"We'd like to see the churches open up their archives to see what information they have about these allega-

tions," he said.

The UN-affiliated group became involved in the issue of residential schools in Canada in response to complaints from former students who felt they have been unable to get justice under Canadian law. The federal government, with the support of the country's leading churches, set up more than 80 residential schools for native children over the past century in all most every province in Canada. Officials estimate that up to 125,000 native children passed through the system before it was closed down in the mid 1960s.

114

Chapter Four: Meanwhile, Back on Campus: Sabotage and Intrigue in the Hallowed Halls of Learning

"You have a very dangerous research topic, and people have spoken to me about it. I would be very careful in your thesis work, if I were you."

Prof. Patricia Vertinsky, Head of Department of Educational Studies, University of B.C., to the author, March, 1996

It was a saving grace for me that, as the nightmare of these crimes was bursting into my life and denying me sleep every night, I was engaged in a graduate studies program at the University of B.C., far from the intrigue and suffering I was immersed in with the residential schools investigation.

As one door is closed in life, another tends to open. And, fortunately for my future and my sanity, the academic world began opening to me as my life in the United Church was being systematically destroyed.

After our family was forced to move from Port Alberni in the summer of 1995, my ex-wife Anne and I both enrolled at the University of B.C. in Vancouver: she to obtain a teaching certificate, and I to pursue a doctoral degree in native studies. I wanted to learn more about what I had been through, and about the residential schools' hidden history. But even more basically, I wanted a break from all the madness.

I knew and loved the University of B.C. campus, in whose forest-ringed quiet I had spent my adolescent years. So it was only natural that I return there to sort out and build a new life for my family and I, now that my old one had been ruined.

Years before, I had nearly followed an academic career on the same campus after I completed a Master's degree in Political Science, but I had given that up to pursue the ministry and work in the United Church. Now, I figured, I would return to those roots, and "fill in the gaps" of my knowledge about the residential schools in the process. I chose to do my doctoral research on a study of the United Church residential schools in Port Alberni and Ahousaht.

"You could have picked a less controversial thesis topic" my departmental advisor, Professor Jean Barman, joked with me during my first week in the Ph.D. program in Educational Studies. "But I'm glad you didn't."

At that time, in the fall of 1995, the whole topic of Canadian residential schools was still a guarded and unpublicized secret. None of the lawsuits against the churches and federal government had begun at that point, and those parties consequently felt free to deny everything about their crimes. And so my choice of research topics was treated as a curious novelty around the Department; and yet one which raised the hair on some peoples' backs, especially two of the faculty: Patricia Vertinsky and Murray Elliott. The latter, it turned out, was a United Church officer who sat on the very Executive body which voted to "de-list" me the following year!

Naturally, I didn't know this at the time. And while Elliott's presence in the Department would prove to be disastrous for me the next year, when I was denied any funding for my program on his recommendation, it nevertheless helped to illuminate how far the United Church would reach into my life, and the supposedly independent realm of higher learning, in order to scuttle my research into their extremely dirty laundry.

Nevertheless, that research was given a tremendous boost the same year, when UBC obtained from the federal Department of Indian Affairs (DIA) much of their microfilmed records from west coast Indian residential schools. Suddenly, the detailed evidence of atrocities and suffering in these schools was available for anyone to read: letters of Indian Agents, petitions from native chiefs, and residential school records which confirmed all the terrible stories that school survivors were simultaneously sharing with me in downtown eastside healing circles.

The chief American prosecutor at the Nuremburg Trials, Robert Jackson, once commented that oral testimonies about crimes against humanity are convincing, but when such stories are combined with corroborating documents, they become conclusive proof of these crimes. And, in February of 1996, precisely that explosive combination came together in my hands.

Love and Death in the Valley

I remember the moment this fact struck home, soon after I began to scour the DIA archives in the basement of Koerner Library at UBC. I was perusing the records of the United Church's Alberni residential school one morning when a single document suddenly stared out at me: the Application for Admission Form, which every aboriginal parent had to sign under a federal law, and which forced them to surrender guardianship over their own children to the Principal of the school.

That very same week, in early February of 1996, the first class action lawsuit against the United Church and feds had been launched by fifteen survivors of the Alberni school; and the church had made a big splash in the media by declaring that it was the federal government, not themselves, that was responsible, and legally liable, for "abuses" in the residential schools.

The document I discovered proved them wrong.

The damning evidence didn't stop there. I read letters from Indian Agents which admitted that church officers were covering up the many deaths of Indian children in the residential schools, and that they were colluding in this practice. I discovered the report of Dr. Peter Bryce, chief medical inspector for DIA in the early 1900's, which cited an average death rate of over 50% in these "schools", and claimed *"the conditions are being deliberately created in our residential schools to spread infectious disease."* And I read the pathetic, barely literate petitions of native elders all over the west coast which pleaded to the government to stop the violent abuse of their children by missionaries; petitions which were always turned down.

I've never been one to keep secrets very well, so as I learned the hidden history of the residential schools I shared the truth in my doctoral seminar classes, and with my research advisors, Professors Jean Barman and Don Wilson. They were both excited yet wary about what I was discovering.

For one thing, the evidence before me was a flat contradiction of the orthodox academic consensus on the Indian residential schools. The official line—propagated by church, state, media and academia alike—was (and is) that the schools were a supposedly "well intentioned" plan gone awry, and that some random physical and sexual "abuses" had gone on which were beginning to be acknowledged and "compensated."

Everything I was reading in the DIA archives, and hearing from survivors in the native healing circles, said precisely the opposite: namely, that the schools were part of a master plan of systematic ethnic cleansing which resulted in the torture and deaths of countless children, and that none of these crimes were admitted to by the churches and government which perpetrated what was clearly genocide.

I remember using that term in one of Jean Barman's seminars, and watching as the wholly-Caucasian class did a collective wince, as if someone had struck them.

"But that implies deliberate killing" commented Jean.

"That's right" I answered.

Her disapproving look said volumes. My graduate colleagues around the table looked away from me at that moment, just like my fellow ministers had done at the Presbytery gathering when I suggested we travel to the Ahousaht Indian reserve and listen to the people there. I was clearly stepping over the invisible boundary again, and treading where career-conscious souls never go.

Soon after this incident, I took up my dilemma with my other academic advisor, Don Wilson, who was a reclusive and affable fellow with a lot of common sense.

"I feel like I'm being subtly pressured to stay away from the whole topic of the actual history of the residential schools" I told him in his office one evening.

"It's not the topic I would have recommended" he replied. "It's too hot politically these days."

"But that's what makes it so worthy of study" I said, getting excited despite Don's coolness. "The official line says one thing, and the evidence says another. Doesn't that need some scholarly investigation, to establish the truth?".

Don stared at me for awhile and finally said, "Are you here to seek the truth or get a degree, Kevin?"

That was the question. But Don knew the answer even before he asked it, and so his attitude towards me after that was one of an admiring but sad regret.

Love and Death in the Valley

With the same kind of innocence that I had shown in Presbytery years before, I thought then that I could pursue the truth and also earn a degree: have the cake of my own integrity and eat it too, if you like. And I might have been able to do so, if I had chosen another research topic. But God or some other trickster kept leading me into minefields which were not supposed to be triggered: like long-buried children, and churches which profit their corporate partners with stolen native land. And once again I reaped the bitter fruits of the explosions which followed.

The pattern was the same as in the church: I was first given the chance to recant my "heresy" and dangerous wanderings, and return to the fold. The offer came to me shortly after I had announced my research topic, from Professor Patricia Vertinsky, who was the head of the Department. She invited me into her office one morning and put the case to me rather quickly.

"You have a very dangerous research topic and some people have spoken to me about it. I would be very careful in your thesis work if I was you."

The threat was clear, and like a deja vu experience. Shocked, I replied, "Who is my research dangerous to?"

The woman ignored my question and went on.

"I'd like to be kept abreast of your work and how it's progressing. I have to insist that I be a member of your thesis committee."

That was a very odd request, since Vertinsky's area of specialization was completely unrelated to my research field, and at best she'd be a fifth wheel in my work. When I told Don Wilson of her remarks, he turned pale and shook his head.

"That's impossible. Why would she want to sit on your committee?".

"I don't know, but I'd call that interfering with my academic freedom, wouldn't you?" I answered.

Don became very nervous after that, like a man walking on eggshells. It all seemed so familiar: the veiled threat, the gradual distancing of people from me, the suddenly suspicious or embarrassed glances from colleagues. I felt like disaster was gathering its storm cloud around me once again.

Other events in my life at that time only confirmed my forebodings. In the same month that I was threatened by Vertinsky, three things happened all at once:

- the first class action lawsuit by residential school survivors commenced in Nanaimo against the United Church and federal government

- my employer, Comox-Nanaimo Presbytery of the United Church, petitioned its BC Conference to have me permanently expelled and delisted from ministry

- my ex-wife Anne filed for divorce and met with United Church lawyer Iain Benson to obtain confidential church documents which she would use in her subsequent custody battle with me over our two daughters.

In other words, all the sharks closed in for the kill.

Now that I had gone public with native eyewitnesses' claims of murder in their residential schools, and had discovered corroborating documents to back up these stories, the church was out for blood. Their scuttling of my professional career and credibility probably became all the more necessary, in their mind, at that very moment because of the commencing of lawsuits against them which would eventually climb into the thousands.

The church officialdom knew very well how damaging to them was the evidence I held in my hands. And the last thing they wanted was for me to gain the respectability of a Ph.D. One of their own officials even said so.

His name was Murray Elliott, and sadly for me he was a colleague of Patricia Vertinsky's and a senior faculty member in my Department. He was the man who decided which graduate students would be recommended for funding and teaching assistantships. But he was also a permanent member of the Executive of the B.C. Conference of the United Church, which at that very moment was voting to have me permanently expelled from my profession as a minister.

Murray was quite vocal of his opinion of me and my research topic around the Department. A fellow graduate student, a woman named Helen Papuni, told me that spring that Murray had demanded "in a rage" that she remove a newspaper article describing my firing by the church from the door of her office.

"He was acting totally crazy and calling you all sorts of bad names" she told me shortly after that. "He said that you were an unworthy husband and minister, and that you were trying to destroy the church. *But what was worse was he said you would never be allowed to finish your thesis.* I was scared to be in the same room with him, to be honest. He's got a real vendetta going against you and someone should rein him in, 'cause it's a pretty unethical way for a faculty member to be treating a student."

Murray's threat that I would not finish my thesis was no idle boast. The following September, with a grade point average of 88%, I was nevertheless denied any funding from the Department, and my applications for teaching assistantships and graduate fellowship awards were also rejected. Murray was the faculty member responsible for making these decisions about financial aid to students.

When Don Wilson heard the news, he was literally speechless. He finally said, "That's totally bizarre. Students with far lower grades than you have gotten some funding. I've never heard of anything like this happening in our Department before. I'm really alarmed."

And yet his advice to me was a "wait and see" attitude.

"Maybe it's all just a fluke" he remarked. But the fear in his eyes betrayed his words.

I stumbled through the next academic year in a state of poverty, thanks to Murray's sabotage of my funding. Fortunately, I found part-time work at a local museum, but my timetable to complete my final exams was thrown completely off by all the financial stress, and by the agony of having my family destroyed that same year. For in April, a court order obtained by my ex-wife forced my out of my home and away from daily contact with my two daughters, who were my life. I found an apartment near to them, but every day was a labour of pure will to survive.

On top of this nightmare, I was also subjected to the United Church's kangaroo-court delisting trial throughout this same period, and was caught up in a daily battle to save my career and reputation in the face of institutionalized lies.

Nevertheless, in the midst of this hell, I completed all of my course work that year with a first-class grade average. Only the hurdle of my final exams and thesis lay ahead.

Suddenly and cruelly, it all came to naught. In September, 1997, my several applications for funding in the Department were again turned down, as before after decisions made by Murray Elliott. With that, my academic work and career was effectively destroyed, since I couldn't afford that year's tuition of $2,200 without university funding.

In desperation, I turned to Don Wilson that month for help in having my applications reconsidered, but the man was terribly shaken, and suffering from a sudden change of heart. He announced that he was withdrawing as head of my committee.

"I'm taking early retirement next year" he said, his eyes avoiding mine. "I just don't have the time to supervise you anymore."

I lost heart after that. My last faculty supporter having been eliminated, I knew that any chance for funding was gone. But I didn't go down without a fight.

I wrote to the UBC Board of Governors and demanded that they investigate what I termed the *"gross interference by faculty members of the Department of Educational Studies into my academic freedom and research ... and the sabotage of my career by professors possibly acting at the behest of the United Church and other parties."*

Precisely who those "other parties" were was not as obvious or important to me, at that time, as the clear fact that the United Church had once again sabotaged my life and work because of my continued investigation into their crimes. But as the UBC Board of Governors and their spokesman, Dennis Pavlich, refused to act on my request, and eventually whitewashed the entire affair and completely exonerated Vertinsky and Elliott, I had to ask some deeper questions.

It wasn't just the church that stood to lose by my research, but the very corporate funders that keep UBC afloat: namely, MacMillan-Bloedel, Weyerhauser, Interfor and the other logging multinationals whose CEO's have served as the Chancellor, President and other senior officers of the University, and whose largesse has built much of the campus.

And there was the dreadful irony: the very corporation—MacMillan-Bloedel—whose ties with the United Church, and profiting off stolen native land, had caused my expulsion from ministry, was once again at the centre of my professional annihilation.

"Big Timber runs this province, Kev" commiserated one of my friends after he learned of the ending of my Ph.D. studies. "It runs the church and the university. Why should you be surprised by what happened to you?".

I wasn't, really. For my research topic was not ultimately about murdered native children but the colonial triangle of church, state and corporate power that still rules British Columbia, and whose machinations were clearly laid bare by my discovery of the Ahousaht land deal.

The lucrative Lot 363, after all, had been the site of the United Church's Ahousaht Residential School, where generations of native kids had been brutalized and murdered. MacMillan-Bloedel's land grab of this valuable property was as much put in jeopardy by the contents of my thesis as the church's own tattered credibility.

As I discovered, the residential schools were simply one tactic by a gang of European robbers of how to secure aboriginal lands and resources. And that theft is still going on.

All of this came home to me with a vengeance after I had to drop out of my doctoral program. I was outraged that the church and its friends were once again able to reach out and destroy my livelihood and efforts to uncover the truth. But "**That which does not destroy me only strengthens me**." And this latest assault only doubled my resolve to uncover the truth about church-sponsored genocide.

And so, as 1998 began, I threw myself into unlocking the evidence of such crimes held in the DIA archives which, until then, I had approached merely as a resource for my thesis material. I began spending entire days in the Koerner Library basement, becoming a familiar occupant of the microfilms section to the staff, one of whom even jokingly suggested to me that I move a bed into the stacks.

It was all for a purpose more obvious to me every day. For, as I've related, in February of 1998, our aboriginal healing circles in downtown Vancouver sponsored the first public meeting into genocide in residential schools; and from that event we organized the June, 1998 IHRAAM Tribunal, whose judges were to rely so heavily on the documents I was unearthing from the UBC archives every day.

I would never have been able to play such a fundamental role in the Tribunal and these other public exposures of the residential school crimes if I had have been comfortably ensconsed in a doctoral program and academic career. So, I am almost thankful for all of the garbage the church and its cronies have put me through, for with each new attack on me, the guilty ones were simply laying the basis for their own demise. Every one of their plots to silence me and the native eyewitnesses has simply boomeranged back against them.

You'd think they'd get the message by now!

I received little human consolation or support during this terrible time. I was suddenly divorced, penniless, and abandoned by everyone, save for a few family members. Looking back, I don't really understand how I stood up under the repeated blows. But one of my unexpected sources of strength then were the long-dead voices from the DIA archives I was studying every day. They helped to answer the riddle of how, and why, religious bodies armed by the state can destroy innocent children with such an easy conscience and lawful powers—and continue to perpetrate their terror on anyone who would challenge them.

"Please help our people. Mr. Ross is not a missionary but a police man. He arrest and harm our chiefs and cause much damage here."

These desperate, scribbled words of some unknown scribe a century ago introduced me to the answer. They were part of a petition of a group of Ahousaht native elders to the government in 1905 that described a reign of terror being perpetrated among their people by a Presbyterian missionary named John Ross.

In the nearly-faded photocopies, I discovered that John Ross had been sent among the Ahousahts in 1903 with special powers—that of the church and state rolled into one person. The government had made Ross a magistrate, and given him the authority to hold special courts and form a private force of native constables to arrest any Ahousaht who potlatched, drummed or conducted any traditional ceremonies.

With such powers, Ross arrested any of the chiefs who wouldn't surrender their land or send their children to the residential school he established on the property his grandson, Hamilton Ross, would one day buy at a bargain price from the United Church—Lot 363. Like Catholic missionaries throughout the world, John Ross set up a

Love and Death in the Valley

theocratic dictatorship among the Ahousaht people, confident that his church and government were behind him.

They were indeed. As with his Methodist colleague Alfred Stone, who ran the Port Renfrew region with an iron hand, Ross received the unconditional backing of the government Indian Agent, even when his actions resulted in the harming and deaths of children. At least two native children died from drugs dispensed by John Ross in 1905, according to elders, and yet the Indian Agent wrote in response, "I am convinced that Principal Ross was in no wise (sic) at fault for the deaths of these children ... The Siwash (Indians) here are always cooking up complaints against Ross because of his role in enforcing the laws prohibiting the potlatching."

And yet the complaints against Ross continued. Even non-native inhabitants of the region accused Ross of extorting money from Indians, running blackmarket opations in stolen native goods, and personally administering public floggings to "troublesome" chiefs who wouldn't attend church.

But like all dreams of empire, Ross' plan went askew. In 1915, the daughter of one of Ross' arch-enemies was found dead at the residential school, and Ross resigned from his post the next day. The death of yet another native child was not unusual at the Ahousaht school—half of the students there, on average, died every year from tuberculosis and other diseases—but Carrie George was the daughter of the chief who had fought Ross the hardest and refused to surrender his territory to Ross. Even while exonerating him, the Indian Agent implied that Ross was leaving under a cloud of suspicion of having murdered the girl.

The United Church of Canada inherited the land that Ross had wrested from the Ahousahts, and one day sold it to Ross' grandson— a story that was told to me by the murdered girls' grand-nephew: Chief Earl George. But try as it could, the church couldn't completely eradicate the memory of Carrie's death, or that of so many other children, despite the solid backing and protection it was receiving from the government.

The John Ross story helped me to understand my own situation, and the ease with which the United Church had destroyed my livelihood not just once, but twice—even reaching within the halls of academia to do so. It also explained why the federal government was bending over backwards to accept responsibility for the residential schools when the lawsuits began, and in this way to cover for the churches. It was the same old game of state-sanctioned cover-up and exoneration, only this time waged not in lonely Indian reserves but across the nation.

This cover-up was typified by the thorough misinformation campaign about the residential schools which the church began constructing across the country at this time, with the help of the state-run CBC and major media. The stakes were high, and no-one was to be allowed to know the hidden history that survived in fragments in the records I was examining, and in the voices I was hearing every week in healing circles.

I'd often rest my eyes after hours of squinting at faded documents, and wonder how in God's name I was to let the world know what went on in these Christian death camps, when I was up against the combined forces of the churches and government that had pulled off this Holocaust. I ended up realizing that quoting the odds wasn't my business; simply documenting and telling what I knew was. And nothing in creation was going to stop me from doing so.

One advantage of being on the bottom, of having had virtually everything stripped from you, is that you have the freedom to consecrate yourself. After I was forced out of my doctoral program, nothing stood in the way of me devoting my life to revealing this hidden Holocaust. I became completely absorbed in what would eventually become The Truth Commission into Genocide in Canada.

That's not to say that it was an entirely healthy decision, on a personal level. Worthy and necessary, absolutely. But inwardly, my feeling was this: *My life is a write-off, so I might as well sacrifice it for a good cause.* I didn't worry anymore about "healing" myself, regaining a career or becoming "respectable" again. None of that mattered anymore, nor did it seem even remotely possible. After all, hadn't the United Church officer who had fired me, Art Anderson, warned my ex-wife, **"Kevin will never work again in this province unless he plays ball"?**

No, I couldn't do much about the slaughter that powerful men had foisted on me, or on people like Harriett Nahanee and Carrie George; but I could undermine their lies and expose their crimes with the simple truth that lay in my hands. Or, put another way, as Union

Love and Death in the Valley

Colonel John Buford had exclaimed prior to the valiant stand of his battalion against overwhelming odds at the battle of Gettysburg in 1863, "We are few in number, but we can deny them the high ground!".

Such a stand was my only consolation, and my one sure and true weapon in a clearly "hopeless battle".

This was the determination that helped give birth to the IHRAAM Tribunal, and allowed the genocide of a gentle people to be made public for the first time in our history. It was forged from suffering; but from out of it has come, even in the midst of betrayal, that most rare of gifts: hope.

Interlude: On Fear and its Children, and other Banalities

Having twice suffered such an up-close trashing of my livelihood and hopes in the same number of years, I have gained a few insights into the power of fear when generated by those in authority, and the absurdities and wrongs which otherwise decent people feel compelled to engage in as a result.

Three examples come to mind.

John Abma's Farm:

One of the backroom actors in my expulsion from my Port Alberni parish was John Abma, a rotund Dutch farmer from mid Vancouver Island. John was the nominal head of Comox-Nanaimo Presbytery during the time that body fired me, although the sad fellow was merely a "lay delegate" who worried more about the overhead on his dairy farm than church matters.

Like Bob Stiven and the other ministers who were lined up to "testify" against me at my defrocking, John Abma was set up to do the dirty work of powerful men elsewhere. And, like the others, he didn't seem to recognize the role he was playing.

That's not to say he didn't like playing it. Abma's job was to prepare my congregation for the axe that was about to fall just before my removal, according to Gerry Walerius and others who told me of those events. And he did so with a passion that was out of place in his bovine demeanour.

John was clearly on a religious crusade when he spoke to the secret board meeting of my church in mid-January, 1995, to which I was not invited.

"Kevin has to go!" he thundered at my parishioners.

Someone had the temerity to ask him why.

"He wants my farm!" the poor guy blurted out, to the confused stares of the gathered faithful.

"My farm!" he repeated to the silent onlookers. "He wants to sell my farm and give it away to the poor!"

Abma paused and said, trying to be calm, "Well, that's what he's been preaching here, right? That we should all give everything we have to a bunch of welfare bums?".

Whenever I get around to suing the United Church for their terrorizing of me, I have it in mind to make as one of my non-negotiable demands that I be given John Abma's farm, so that I can personally parcel it out to the most undeserving and destitute people I know—the ones who so obviously haunt John's nightmares.

Gee, I can hardly wait!

Brian Thorpe's Moral Challenges:

Whether smelling of cow shit or mere banality, functionaries tend to do the same dance: There's always someone they're afraid of who's telling them to do something they know is wrong ... but they nevertheless do it anyway.

Which brings us to Mr. Thorpe.

For awhile in his dealings with me, the timid-faced church bureaucrat acted much like a messenger boy, relaying decisions or procedures to me as I struggled to formally appeal each latest assault from the church through "official channels". But I soon discovered that he in fact was the architect of much of the garbage I was going through, in league with his lawyer buddy Jon Jessiman, who arranged my firing and defrocking.

The depth to which Thorpe was personally sinking to drive me from the church and shred my reputation became suddenly clear to me on September 3, 1997, at a press conference I held outside the United Church's B.C. Conference office in Vancouver.

The incident was caught on film, unfortunately for both Thorpe and his string-puller, Mr. Jessiman. A Cable TV news crew was videoing the event, which was my release to the media of archival documents proving that the United Church had been the legal guardian of all native kids in their residential schools as far back as 1942, and hence were legally liable for the crimes and damages there.

This was explosive stuff, and solid evidence for the native folks who were suing the United Church and the feds at that very moment in a much-publicized class action lawsuit in Nanaimo. The documents I gave to the press destroyed the church's argument that it wasn't liable for the residential school"abuses". And both Thorpe and Jessiman knew it.

They were frightened men that day. Peering out at me through the thick glass of the Conference office, they didn't seem to know what to do at first. And I was too preoccupied with talking to reporters to notice what they finally did.

A student friend of mine from UBC, Caleb Sigurgeirson, told me about it first.

"Those two guys from the church just took stuff out of your briefcase, Kevin"

Caleb exclaimed angrily. "They did it when you weren't looking."

I went over to my case, and sure enough the folder that carried the original copies of the incriminating documents had disappeared.

"Who did it?" I asked Caleb.

"The littler guy, but the fat one was watching the whole thing from the doorway."

Laughing in disbelief, I said, "But they're the two top officials of the United Church in B.C. They wouldn't steal stuff in public!"

I walked into the Conference office and found Thorpe in the photocopy room with my material.

"I'd like the documents back that you took out of my case" I said to him.

"I don't have them!" Thorpe blurted out, trying to conceal the papers.

"If you don't give them back to me I'll tell what happened to the CBC reporters outside" I replied.

Jessiman suddenly loomed out of the background, like some lumbering potentate. He announced, "Never mind Brian, it doesn't matter. Give them back to him."

Thorpe sheepishly handed over some unstapled papers, only some of the original documents.

When I returned to the street, a Cable Four reporter approached me and said that he had caught the incident on film.

Sure enough, the film clip shows Jessiman standing in the Conference office doorway, watching as Thorpe approaches my briefcase hesitantly. Thorpe turns, almost symbolically, to look at his lawyer boss for instructions, and Jessiman nods. Thorpe then reaches down and removes the documents from my case, and then hurries back into the building, as Jessiman looks on and even holds the door open for Thorpe.

The next day, I went to the Vancouver Police with the film clip and an affidavit from Caleb, and attempted to charge Jessiman and Thorpe with theft.

The cops took five months to decide what to do, but finally Crown Counsel Garth Gibson told me to my face that "a theft had definitely occurred" (no shit, Sherlock!), but that "it isn't in the public interest to pursue this complaint."

I asked Mr. Gibson (who worked for the same Attorney-General, Ujjal Dosanjh, who refused to investigate my farcical delisting trial) who, exactly, defined what the "public interest" was. He replied, "I do."

From the horse's mouth, as they say.

The Final Solution:

And that's the way things stay secret, and corrupted, most of the time: a series of gentlemens' agreements among the elite, whether Crown Counsels or church lawyers, to protect the criminals and suppress the truth.

It's enough to make most people throw up their hands in despair and retire to their own little worlds, which is of course what the Old Boys want. But fortunately, some of us don't give up. And some of us are young, and thus more willing to take risks.

For such brave souls is reserved a Final Solution by the Old Boys, when the normal arrangements fail: brute force.

It happened to some friends of mine from a Saanich high school in the spring of 2000. They made the mistake of trying to speak about genocide in residential schools to other young people at the United Church's Annual Meeting in Victoria.

And they were physically assaulted for it by "good Christians".

Nicolle and four of her friends had invited me to speak at their school about the deaths of native children, before two hundred of their peers. After my talk, a group of them were so outraged that they were determined to protest outside the upcoming United Church meeting in Victoria.

When they arrived at the event, however, Nicolle suggested they go into the Annual Meeting rather than picket outside, since it was being held in a public gymnasium and was open to anyone. The five of them, all young women aged sixteen or seventeen, promptly went inside and sat down with the United Church youth delegates, sharing with them material about the "hidden Holocaust" of native people that their church was responsible for.

"We were only there a few minutes when this big guy came over and grabbed me on my shoulder" Nicolle told me later. "He and two other men hauled us up out of our chairs and dragged us over to the door. My arm got twisted and bruised."

"It turns out they were church officials and the big guy said we weren't allowed on the premises." I said back to him, 'Why not? This is a free country and I have the right to be here under the Charter of Rights and Freedoms.'

"Then he said to me, 'The Charter of Rights doesn't apply here. We're the United Church of Canada. Now get out and stay out!'".

I tried to console Nicolle by telling her that essentially the same thing had been done to me since January, 1995, by the same kind of people who had assaulted her.

"But how do they get away with it?" she lamented.

Indeed.

....

Love and Death in the Valley

Chapter Five: What Cannot be Healed, or Spoken: After the Inquisition

"This is what the Lord says: 'Your wound is incurable, your injury beyond healing'".

Jeremiah 30:12

"Christianity sounds like a wonderful idea. Somebody should try it sometime."

George Bernard Shaw

Let's face it, my life had become a disaster after my expulsion from the church and the university, and the sabotage of the residential schools Tribunal. But I didn't realise it until the dust had settled from the tumult of the previous four years, and I could finally become quiet again and really look at myself.

I had had so much of my heart and my life torn away from me that I couldn't move, or think, without my whole self aching. I had become like the battered street people I used to minister to from a safe distance. And, like them, there seemed to be no way out for me.

I still had my own soul, of course, unlike the defeated clergy who perjured themselves under oath when they lied about me at my delisting trial. And that pearl of myself, of course, is ultimately all that matters. But between that recognition and the rest of my life, there lay a vast battlefield strewn with the dead and the dying, and by the fall of 1998 I found myself quite alone in that wasteland with no supplies or ammunition left.

When he was just nineteen, and part of the Third Canadian Division's assault on Vimy Ridge during World War One, my grandfather was wounded by German bullets, and he almost died. Grandpa told me that being shot didn't hurt him at all. It was only after he fell into a shell crater that he felt his pain, because he expected his arms and legs to move, and they wouldn't, no matter what he did.

Love and Death in the Valley

I kept trying to move myself past the traumas of those years, but my limbs wouldn't respond. It felt like they had been hacked right off. I didn't realise the extent of my wounds until I was quiet and alone in the forest one day, and it was then that I saw the gaping holes in me, and I knew they were incurable, because they were not my wounds alone.

The words of Rabbi Abraham Heschel came alive to me then, when he described a condition such as mine as being part of the "divine agony" that the prophet shares with the Creator, and all of humanity:

> *"We and the prophet have no language in common. To us, the state of the world seems fair and correctable; to the prophet it is a nightmare. Our conscience is soothed and confined, and we sleep well amidst slaughter; but the prophet can never slumber, for God and the suffering ones do not rest.*
>
> *"The prophet's ear perceives the silent sigh; the prophet's heart shares the divine agony. For, unlike the rest of us, the prophet holds together God and humanity in a single thought."* **(The Prophets,** 1962)

I did not visualise what I was doing in Port Alberni in such terms when I was there, but looking back, all that I preached and did was like expressing God and the people around me in a single, pure thought. I saw no difference between Jesus, in his terrible struggle to be true, and the people in the pews, or myself. There was no separation between Caucasians and natives, rich or poor, or men and women in my heart, and I tried expressing that by breaking down those illusory walls in my own congregation.

This scandalous effort is a single, true thought from the mind of God that cannot be theologised, analysed, objectified or turned into an item on the monthly church board agenda. It simply is.

Ministers have the choice every day to live in the light of that "I am", and allow it to change them, as their Master advised; or to try to harness that rainbow onto the well-oiled but dead machine that is the Christian church, and kill both it and themselves.

It is not an easy choice to make, for we lose everything we hold dear in the process. Frankly, it seems to be beyond the courage and the love of most of us. These days, I feel it has moved beyond my battered abilities, as much as I long for the return of that choice. But between the summers of 1992 and 1995, I was able to make the choice to stand and grow in that light, in a place where it was needed more than life itself, or food, or bigger church attendance: in a sideshow town called Port Alberni.

Perhaps it is given to us to make the choice only once in our lifetime, at the crossroads moment that must be waited and watched and bled for so we don't miss the chance to leap. If so, then I have done my duty. But even veterans of the wars can long for one more chance to see everything arrayed as it truly is, and see themselves as they truly are, resplendent and clear, and ready again to be the arm of the great Mystery in the battle that never ends.

Knowing in my soul what was approaching, I tried to put this message into my last sermon I preached at St. Andrew's, on January 22, 1995, the day before my firing. I ended my words by saying this:

"Like Jesus when he was twelve, we are each searching for our 'true father', for the completeness of God, even if we are not conscious of this urge. That search tugs at our hidden heart and compels us to look beyond the disappointments and narrowness of our present lives, and of our present church.

"But we cannot begin this search here, within these four walls we like to call 'St. Andrew's United Church', for in here does not reside our true view. The open, sunlit panorama that beckons to each of us, and to us as a church, lies only and always through other people, especially those who struggle for justice, and for food. We can be as reconciled as we like to one another in this room, or in this church, but that union will not lead us to God. For reconciliation is only a <u>consequence</u> of first doing what is right in God's mind—of actually being just and honest people.

"We in the United Church cannot call for justice with lips twisted by lies; we will never heal with hands stained in blood. First we must be free of our selves, of our own bloody history, confessing that <u>we</u> are the ones who crucified Jesus, and six million other Jews, and ninety million native Indians, and so many other innocents.

"Perhaps it is too late. Perhaps we are what Martin Luther King described when he referred to the white church in America: 'an

Love and Death in the Valley

irrelevant social club with no meaning for the twentieth century.' A church under a final judgement."

I believe that the United Church of Canada, along with the other churches which exterminated native children and then buried them and the truth, are under a final judgement. They have been exposed as the enemy of what they profess. And, like the prophet Jeremiah observed, there is no cure for their sickness, for it is spiritual in nature.

It took me some years to learn this terrible fact, after much hard experience within the church. But that experience does not lie. And I began to acquire it only one year after my ordination.

Now that Christ has become Caesar: My First Taste of the Real Church

After I was ordained, in the spring of 1990, I did a brief stint on the prairies, like many novice clergy. My assignment was three tiny United Churches in the very southwest corner of Manitoba, in the deep and dying flatland where families cling to their farms and their churches for dear life. Those families were basic and good people, typical prairie stock. But after a year in Pierson, Manitoba, a job opened up for me in the United Church's largest urban mission, in downtown Toronto, and I leapt at the chance to follow what I felt was my real calling, as a minister among the poorest of the poor.

The job was director of urban ministry and chaplain at Fred Victor Mission on Queen street, the oldest church project among the poor in Canada, that started as a Methodist soup kitchen in the latter 19th century. The name said much: "Fred Victor" was Fred Victor Massey, one of the four original sons of the Massey dynasty who died of tuberculosis as a young man, and in whose memory the Masseys have poured mountains of cash into the United Church.

Nearly fifty people applied for the job, but I was quickly short-listed because of my extensive work on Vancouver's skid row with First United Church. After a personal interview, in February, 1991, I was unanimously chosen for the position. And so our family said our sad goodbyes to the Manitoba congregations which had welcomed us so warmly, and we motored off to Toronto by that summer.

"Freddie's", as the locals call it, is a jumble of offices and low-income housing which sits astride some of the most valuable real estate in Canada, a few blocks east of Yonge street. It is the United Church's largest urban mission, a $30 million a year operation and a huge tax write-off for its clutch of wealthy patrons. And yet on all sides, homeless and forgotten people try to survive, and often stumble and die. And sometimes they are washed ashore into the Mission.

I was hired to be a clergyman for these people. The Mission Director, a portly minister named Paul Webb who was close to retirement, gave me that mandate the day I was hired.

"We've been lacking a religious aspect to our work" Webb told me, through dull, thick glasses. "Sure, we provide housing and advocacy for the poor, but they need more. We've lost the spirit, and we hope you'll bring it back to us."

There had been no chaplain at the Mission for many years, and the place reeked of desperate lives and uninspired, routine-minded staffers like Webb, who huddled with his colleagues every day in small basement offices, quite cut off from the poor people who frequented the street-level drop-in centre. And so I spent my first weeks at Freddie's getting to know everyone, upstairs and downstairs.

As I would encounter later in Port Alberni, two different worlds sat alongside each other at the Mission, each a solitude: downstairs were desk-bound social activists who saw the world through paper; upstairs struggled men and women looking for some small peace and rest before the next wave pushed them under for good. Neither world was aware of the other, and I knew that a space was needed in which the two could meet. And so I began to hold open worship services in the Mission's lounge, twice every week.

This circle became what the Loaves and Fishes food bank was later in my Port Alberni church: it opened the door to hidden stories and crushed lives, and gave both a chance to speak—to the shock and horror of the United Church officialdom. But it also gave me my first insight into the real, rather than the imagined, nature of that church, as a large and money-ruled corporation.

Our first service was held in September of 1991, and nearly sixty people filled the room: all of them poor, either housing residents or street people. We didn't have Bibles, hymn books or even musical instruments, since I was given no budget by Paul Webb, but our service lasted more than two hours. One by one, people prayed aloud, shared their own stories, and struggled with how to deal with the terrible poverty and homelessness in the neighbourhood.

We called our group "The Upper Room Church", since Carole Boutin, a former street person who was an early member, reminded us that it was in a place like ours that Jesus appeared to his friends after everyone thought he had been killed. The title seemed to fit. By Christmas, nearly a hundred people were coming to The Upper Room, and we had to move into a larger hall in the building.

None of the Mission staff ever came to our gatherings, including Paul Webb, except during our Christmas service, when we provided dinner. I kept urging Webb, especially, to attend so that he could hear firsthand from the people he was supposed to be serving what they wanted, and who they were. But Webb regularly begged off, with the same nervous look in his eyes.

Nevertheless, our services slowly began giving people the confidence to speak out, and take small steps to change things. Two of our earliest members, Mike Waffel and Ron Payne, had been trying to improve the housing conditions and rights of their fellow Mission tenants for many months, against the intransigence of staff and church officers. Our Biblical readings and personal reflections suddenly took on a relevant but risky tone when Mike and Ron rose to speak.

"My religion is justice" Mike Waffel said confidently one Sunday morning in October, 1991. "You can believe whatever gets you through the night, but I believe we're here to improve life for our neighbours. And our neighbours here in this building are being put through hell."

Mike went on to describe a regime of terror in the Mission's "Keith Witney" housing. Tenants were being evicted by the staff for such "infractions" as having a guest after nine o'clock at night, or lending a key to a friend. Rents were often raised without warning, in violation of the Landlord-Tenant Act, and bribes to staff to avoid such increases were expected, and commonplace. Anyone who complained about this arrangement was summarily thrown into the street and made homeless.

Even worse, drug dealing and prostitution were rampant throughout Fred Victor Mission and Keith Witney housing, and violence was endemic.

"I'm afraid to be alone at night, in case I get robbed again" said Phil, a retired man in his seventies. "The pimps bring their girls into the housing and they do their tricks in here 'cause they know the cops won't come into a United Church mission. They threaten us if we say anything. Everyone on staff knows about it and they all look the other way."

"Why wouldn't they?" added Mike Waffel. "It's the staff who are dealing the drugs and taking payments from the pimps, even senior staff."

All of this was going on at the most "famous" United Church mission in the country: a place which was regularly praised in the church magazine, *The Observer*, but where in reality church offerings were being regularly spent on drugs, and to aid and abett criminals.

As Phil and Mike and other witnesses spoke, each lending his courage to the other, their eyes invariably turned towards me, as if asking what I was going to do about it all. Victoria Wilson was even more explicit.

Victoria was a large Jamaican woman who was a bedrock of our congregation.

After listening to several weeks of horror stories about the Mission, she stood up and said quietly, "I pray every time we're together that our Lord Jesus will come and save us. I've been praying like that my whole life. Now I see that we have to become his arms and legs and mouth, right here, right now. We have to confront Satan because he's grown up right under our noses, in the church."

That sobered all of us, and I remember sitting in silence with the others for awhile after Victoria spoke, for we all realised the step that was needed next.

And yet perhaps it is inherent in us frail mortals to procrastinate and find reasons not to act, even when the evil is right in front of us. Our group of already-besieged souls would not have done anything to confront the terror at the Mission, I believe, if our neighbours had not have begun dying on our very doorstep. For with the coming of Christmas and the falling temperature, the homeless people of Jarvis and Queen street began dropping and never arising. And that was the trigger that propelled us to arms.

In early December, the first local residents began dying of exposure in freezing snowdrifts and behind convenience store dumpsters. I began meeting many homeless people then, for every night I trekked the downtown alleys with soup and blankets, along with others from our church, and sought out the dying. But we missed saving some friends of ours: Walt and Mary, a homeless couple in their fifties who were members of our church, and who were found dead in each others' arms in a park not a block from where we worshipped.

We held a small memorial service for the two of them on December 8, and during our sharing time, Carol suggested we occupy a downtown church to force them to open their doors to the homeless.

"Our people are dying!" she screamed, in tears. "Mary was my friend and the kindest person you'd ever meet. She didn't deserve what happened to her. How can those churches stay bolted shut every night? Our lives are more important than some fucking church building!"

I regret now that I suggested, instead, that we write an open letter to the downtown churches, and ask them to voluntarily open their doors. I still believed then that church Christians care about lives other than their own enough to respond to such a plea. But the others in our group trusted me, and so we penned our letter and mailed it out to fifty two churches before Christmas.

It was a mild and reasonable call for help. It asked local church members and clergy how they could be worshipping the homeless family of Bethlehem while ignoring other homeless souls on their very doorsteps. It asked them to open their doors, and join with us in our nightly street patrols to "seek out the lost".

Not a single church answered our letter.

It did evoke a response, however, from Mission Director Paul Webb. He was outraged; not at the deaths around us, but at our supposedly "offending" local churches. And what really upset Webb was the fact that we had stated in our letter, *"We don't want your money. We want your presence, with us every night as we meet the homeless on our streets."*

"How could you say such a thing as 'We don't want your money'?" he asked me, horrified that we would shun the golden calf like that, publicly. "Don't you know we're right in the middle of a pledge drive here at the Mission?"

Hoping that he might be joking, I said, "We're not undercutting your work, Paul. It's just that people we know have been dying from the cold ..."

"You're to issue a retraction of your letter right away" he barked at me, with unusual passion.

"It's a group letter" I answered. "Our entire congregation wrote and signed it. I can't go around them."

"You'll have to, if you want to keep your job" he retorted.

I said nothing for a moment, and then asked him, "What's going on?"

Webb was worked into a real lather, and he said quickly, "I've been thinking of placing you in another position anyway, Kevin, at the Bathurst street housing project. It pays more and is a better place for you."

I could only stare at him, quite dumbfounded.

"We've heard some disturbing things being said at your worship services by Ron Payne and Mike Waffel. I don't know if you know that they're both in serious trouble with the law. You can't believe what they say about things going on in here."

"It isn't just Mike and Ron who are saying it" I answered. "Lots of tenants talk about drug dealing and prostitution, and describe being forced to pay bribes to staff members ...".

"Pure lies" Webb seethed, rising up. "Why do you listen to such crap?"

"So everyone is just making all that up? For what reason?" I said.

Webb quickly stood up and opened the door to his office, saying gravely, "You can go now."

That conversation occurred on December 22, 1991. Things began happening quickly after that:

On December 28, I was told by memo that our worship services could no longer be held anywhere in the Mission. The same communique said that my job was to be reviewed immediately (even though my contract stated that such a review would occur only after one year, and I had been working at Freddie's barely five months), and I faced "possible disciplinary action", for no stated reason.

Love and Death in the Valley

The next day, as I was deciding how to respond to this blow, one of our group members, Mike Burca, met me in the Mission drop-in with a happy look on his face.

"You should see what I uncovered, Kev" he said quietly. Mike had worked as a policeman in Romania, and saw himself as a cloak and dagger type. But he also worked as a computer programmer for the Mission, and as such had access to its financial records. He drew me aside and handed me a long sheet of paper.

"What's that?" I asked tiredly, for I hadn't slept much the previous night.

"The left-hand column is this year's official budget, the one everyone got in the Annual Report. The right-hand column is the Mission's actual budget. They don't match."

Sure enough, a discrepancy of more than $880,000 stared out at me from the crumpled page. Urban Ministry was alloted $50,000, according to one column; but I had been told that there were no funds available for my work, beyond my salary. I had had to make special requisitions from General Accounts to even procure a few Bibles for our worship circle. So where had that $50,000 gone?

"Somebody's embezzling a lot of dough" said Mike triumphantly.

"Has anyone seen this?" I asked him.

"Sure" he said. "Webb, Linda Davidson, the whole senior staff. I even sent one to Paul Mills, the Chairman of the Board. But I'm not waiting for them. I'm going to the Mounties."

Mike Burca never showed up at the Mission after that. He suddenly lost his job and was barred from the premises. But I ran into him during our nightly street walks among the homeless in early January, and he told me that the RCMP had refused to investigate the Mission.

"That constable I talked to must be a United Church member" Mike told me, as we warmed ourselves over a hot air grate on which seven people slept. "He said there was no way a church would be embezzling money and I should back right off."

Ron Payne and Mike Waffel were also thrown out of the Mission that same week, being evicted without cause on January 1. Their application to have the United Church brought before the Landlord-Tenant arbitrator was denied. Their appeals to the RCMP to investigate drug dealing and prostitution at the Mission were repeatedly ignored, in an echo of the Mounties' later refusal to investigate crimes by United Church officers at Indian residential schools in B.C.

As more of our members were evicted, or lost Mission-funded jobs or office space, I knew it was time for me to do something, and take things to a higher level. I documented all the evidence of wrongdoing at the Mission, including Webb's attacks against myself and others who had voiced the wrongs, and sent it in letters to the then-Moderator of the United Church, Walter Farquharson, to national and local church officials, and to the Mission's Chairman of the Board, a Bay street lawyer named Paul Mills. I asked these officials to investigate the Mission and conduct an impartial review of my ministry.

No church official ever responded to my letter, including the Moderator. But the Board Chairman, Paul Mills, called me up immediately and asked me to meet him at his Bay street law office.

His place had a great view of Lake Ontario and the downtown core, and I imagined it was like that lofty pinnacle that another man was taken to, where he was offered the entire world in exchange for something.

Paul Mills stared at me like I was an illegal alien when I entered his office, and he said right away, "Who else has seen that letter you sent me?"

"The people it's copied to, right on the letter" I answered.

"You haven't sent it to the newspapers?"

I asked him why he thought I'd have done that.

Mills didn't answer me, but continued.

"We've known about those allegations for some time. The issue for us is the fact that you wrote a letter about it."

I was dumbfounded, again.

"You mean, you _know_ that those things are going on at the Mission? The embezzling, the drugs? What have you done about it?"

Mills said nothing, but stared at me coldly. I continued, "Paul Webb said that it was all lies, that none of it was going on. But you're saying it is?"

"Like I said, the only problem here is that you wrote a letter about it."

Love and Death in the Valley

I didn't know what to say or think until the lawyer said slowly, "Don't you understand what you're dealing with here?"

And then I did know, quite clearly. I looked out at the vast wealth surrounding us, the opulent skyscrapers from where the country, and the church, are run, and I suddenly knew.

I turned and left Mills' office. There was nothing left to do.

The following week, I tendered my resignation to the Mission. A "negative report" about me was forwarded to the church in British Columbia, where my family and I were bound, prior to my next posting in Port Alberni.

Years later, during the trial that expelled me forever from the church, letters castigating me and demanding my defrocking were obtained by church lawyers from, not surprisingly, both Paul Mills and Mission Director Paul Webb, who had been caught in such miserable lies and corruptions. But their solicited lies form part of the church's "official record" about me.

Mills' parting words to me were strangely akin to those of Fred Bishop in Port Alberni, when he first threatened me, a few years later:

"You're forgetting where you are, Kevin. There are rules in any group and you're not playing by them".

I violated the club rules when I spoke about the church's accepted and acceptable crimes, whether in a downtown mission or in native residential schools. Paul Mills said it all: **The problem was not that the crimes had occurred and were covered up, but that I had written a letter about it.** For, in the United Church, whether at Fred Victor Mission or in Port Alberni, there are no ultimate wrongs, except one: naming the club secrets.

That, above all else, is the one firm lesson that I have learned in the church.

Perhaps the essential secret that I stumbled over is also the most obvious and explosive one: the fact that the Christian church is not actually the church, but a lie. At a terrible cost, this secret can be spoken; and when, against all the odds, it is uttered, there sprouts up something new and incorruptible, even in as unlikely a place as our own incurable lives.

....

In 1761, a philosopher in England named Peter Annet was destroyed by the church and state of his day for writing a series of "blasphemous" articles which questioned parts of the Bible. He was jailed, displayed in the public stocks, fined into poverty, and hounded into sickness and early death. He was my ancestor.

What got Peter in hot water with the church was a work entitled *"The Free Enquirer"*, which he wrote with a single aim: to use reason to discover whether the Bible made sense and was actually true. Peter published only nine copies of it before the police swooped down and arrested him, and confiscated his works. But one copy, at least, survived, and I am holding its worn cover in my hands as I write this.

Standing in my ancestor's tradition, inheriting his same inquiring mind and desire for truth before all else, I feel his spirit hovering over these brown and faded pages, and speaking to me. For he and I share the same enemy, as he describes:

"We wage war against ecclesiastic fraud, priestly avarice, spiritual tyranny, obstinate bigotry, wild superstition, and presumptuous enthusiasm; and fight under the banner of truth ... The spiritual sword, not the carnal, is our weapon. We will bring to light the hidden works of darkness, ransack all nature to find out truth, and drive falsity to the bottomless pit."

It is no accident that Peter and I have faced the same terrorism from the Christian church. The methods of crushing critics have become more sophisticated in two centuries, but the aim has remained the same: to denigrate, publicly humiliate and vanquish forever those who confront the lie garbed in clerical vestments.

Peter was tried and convicted by the Attorney-General on behalf of the state Anglican church; B.C. government minister and cleric John Cashore helped to arrange my expulsion from the ministry. Peter was imprisoned at hard labour and placed in the public pillory, for people to gawk at and pelt with refuse; I was denied work, thrust into poverty, and pilloried at the only public "delisting" of a United Church minister in history, where the most vile trash and lies were thrown at me. If Peter hung helpless and degraded in that wooden pillory, I have been held up for equal shaming in church-run newspapers, on the internet, and through a smear campaign that has reached into every church and many colleges across Canada.

If anything, the church's methods of annihilating its "heretics" have been honed to a finer edge since Peter's day. Today, people like me can be effectively destroyed by churches and officials lauded for their tolerance, commitment to "justice", and "progressiveness". The Christian left hand is kept utterly removed from the bloody right one; the two-faced god Janus turns only its pleasant and numbing smile to the masses, reserving its terrible jaws for those who know its real nature, and say so.

I have seen, up close and personal, how quickly the "nice Christian" can turn ruthless and intolerant, especially the clergy and full-time officials. The "Richelieu Syndrome" of the destructive, uncontrollable Inquisitor who sanctimoniously and self-deceptively "prays for his victim" seems to take flesh as a matter of principle within the Christian church, which functions, in practice, like an untreated sociopath.

It's easier for one person to change than a whole, mutually-reinforcing group of people, especially when they are convinced—and keep being told—that they are the "people of God".

And that's the whole problem.

"Do you think the church spent all that money to get rid of you just because they panicked, or are stupid?" asked Harriett Nahanee to me during my defrocking.

"That's not it at all. They creamed you for the same reason they murdered Maisie Shaw and all those other innocent children: because they think they're God."

It's true. Only "God" can kill children and defend the murder afterwards. Only "God" can sit across from you and tell lies to your face, and crush you and your family, without a shred of conscience in his eyes. For such a God doesn't have to justify or explain anything. ***His might makes all things right.***

I never realised that my "nice, progressive" United Church was the servant of such a God until He reached out through His acolytes and destroyed my life with the same cold calculation that He used to wipe out untold numbers of native people. And the reason that a survivor of His Inquisition cannot be healed, or find the right words to describe what has happened, is because the Lie stands revealed: The God of Christianity is a warrior deity who even murdered His own son.

Like dysfunctional children do, the offspring of this abusive father leap to his defense, usually with convoluted theologies of "atoning grace" or something like that. It seems that God had no choice but to crucify Jesus—wait for it—because of <u>human</u> sin. Hey, <u>we're</u> to blame, not the violent parent! So think the Christians, like any group of battered children who have never matured enough to break from the familial pattern of denying, enabling and ultimately perpetuating the violence.

And so the brutal cycle goes on, from one scapegoat to the next. The problem is never the abuser, you see, just the victims—whether pale-skinned or aboriginal.

Having been one, I've seen up close the scapegoat's function in Christianity, as a psychological and spiritual "release mechanism" for a bunch of otherwise-decent people who are burdened with worshipping a notion of a pathologically-violent God whose victims are strewn across time and the planet. Repressing the awful truth is the order of the day, whether in or out of church, and soon the pressure must boil over and destroy the illusion and peace of the crowd—unless one, or many, can be found to "bear the sins of the multitude", and thereby allow the Christian herd to rest easily for a little while longer.

It's never this conscious, or acknowledged, of course. The image of that tortured Jew is enough to trigger the ritual. Whenever things go wrong, blame the minister—or the stranger. When God kills our child, or ends our marriage, it can't be God who is doing such evil—for the oppressive father is never in the wrong—so a scapegoat must be offered up. And the greater the pain, the more elaborate the crucifixion rite.

In my case, the depth of denial and suffering in the Old Guard of my St. Andrew's congregation was truly enormous, just like in the church generally. Among the prominent "white" members, who set the tone for the others, I had never seen such a sad and guilt-ridden group of people; a guilt inflamed whenever an aboriginal person stepped through the church door.

Rather than deal with it, the Old Guard buried this shame with an angry resentment at the "intruders". No-one from among them can dare name this disgrace, for it is colossal: they carry the stain of the slaughter their own church and relatives have inflicted on countless innocent people, on the very land they now inhabit and "worship" on.

A special rage and retaliation is reserved for those like myself who dare to name this secret. And the fact that one of their own did so made their sense of betrayal—and violence—all the greater. But in the end nothing, of course, was changed by their crucifixion of me.

The others who had arrived in the congregation by the time of my ending made no impact on the course of events, for they were the intruders, and easily disposed of. But later, when the same dark-skinned strangers began to sue the United Church, the Old-Guard of my congregation began "welcoming" Indians back to church, with pleasant words of "apology" and "healing"—amidst considerable publicity. But this lawyer-concocted charade didn't change anything, either. For the Lie was still being spoken, and the secret shame, and crimes, still lay hidden.

Ironically, then, the perpetrators of the Lie are as incapable of healing from it as are its victims. Have United Church members once talked publicly about their <u>own</u> crimes, and <u>their</u> need to change as a people; like, by taking back their church from the overpaid lawyers and unaccountable officials who now run it like a corporation in damage control? Never. ***For it is always <u>other</u> people who need to change, and "heal".***

For me, this is all part of the wound I carry that will not mend. Any wrong can be overcome, any scar healed, <u>but only if there is first genuine lamentation and sorrow by the perpetrators.</u> There is no such despair among Christians in Canada today, even after the murder and torture of untold numbers of children by their churches stands revealed. And that says it all.

"Crazy Mike", a homeless street corner preacher I knew in the downtown east side of Vancouver, once told me there is only one book in the Bible that is really subversive, and capable of turning the tables on all the status-quo arrangements: The Book of Lamentations.

Mike didn't have a theological degree, but he knew what he was talking about. After I had moved to Port Alberni, he wrote to me these words:

"Lamenting means there's no cheap and safe answer possible. People and institutions are always looking for the easy way out, as if God exists to console us on <u>our</u> terms. Most of the Psalms are like that: 'Help me, O Lord', or 'Strike down my enemy, O Lord'. But in Lamentations, things are over, period. Jerusalem has been gutted, the Temple is a pile of ruins. All the rules and vested interests are blown away, because <u>everything has ended</u>.

So, when we really know this, all there is left to do is lament, which is mourning from your guts for what has been lost and <u>can never be recovered</u>. Like at someone's funeral. And that's the only way that the soul and society can be swept clean and freed so that a new seed can sprout up and start growing.

*"But if nobody laments, the new life can't start. It's asphalted over by all our justifications and arrangements that exist to stop things from ever changing. But one genuine tear of remorse can start a flood that will wash away centuries of wrongdoing and sin. That's why nobody knows how to mourn anymore,—**<u>nobody is allowed to mourn anymore</u>**—because if we did, everything would start changing."*

Amen, "Crazy" Mike!

Rather than mourn, Christians have chosen to paper over their own wounds and pretend that they are not dying as a people and as institutions. They are like the terminal cancer patient who is in a permanent state of denial about his own condition.

Such denial is truly pathological, for Christians even deny their most basic beliefs, in practice. Christianity, if it was ever practiced, would destroy itself, for <u>God</u> <u>incarnate</u> has no need of religions, churches or creeds. God in the flesh simply <u>is</u>, and puts an end to all divisions and class distinctions among people: "You are all One in Christ Jesus". So, to survive, Christian churches—which are big businesses and lucrative careers dependent on exactly such distinctions among people—<u>must deny their foundational theology</u>. Such a contradiction cannot be borne by any sane soul for long without him or her being driven mad—or, more exactly, <u>dissociated</u>.

Realising this one day, everything that happened to me at the hands of the United Church officialdom made perfect sense, for I was in an asylum where the lunatics had literally taken over.

The most successful minister in the church, I found, is the man or woman who can function as an efficient, dissociated personality, regularly professing one thing and practising the opposite. It is the psychically and morally <u>integrated</u> person who causes the most problems as a minister, for thought and deed are one in such souls, and the madness of all the "successful" clergy must continually be exposed by these well-rounded persons.

To put this another way: as Presbytery official Bob Stiven put it so succinctly at my "defrocking" trial:

"When Kevin said he had to put God first, he was being pastorally incompetent."

Like corporate efficiency experts, the United Church is very much obsessed with this notion of "competency". At the Vancouver School of Theology, where I did my training for the ministry, courses are referred to as "competencies", not Biblical Studies, or what have you. The prime emphasis there is on turning out "competent" clergy, not spiritual teachers, or even caring, creative people, or (perish the thought!) social rebels in the tradition of Jesus. And from my experience, to be "competent" in the church one must consistently put the corporate allegiance and interest-groups before God—as Bob Stiven so blatantly exclaimed.

The healthiest thing the churches can do today is to close themselves down: to recognize their own spiritual death. They won't engage in such lamenting, of course, because dissociated personalities cannot realise their own sickness. But it's precisely what the Bible prescribes for spiritually-lost groups of people.

If the churches and those who run them would bother to open their own Bibles, and apply their canon to themselves, they'd encounter voices like Isaiah, Jeremiah, Amos and even Jesus raised against the false religion of their day, and demanding the same thing: that it be shut down.

If you believe the Bible, and the churches, these prophets saw absolutely no hope of redeeming a corrupt and self-serving religion that had turned against God.

To a man, they said the same thing, in the name of a violated deity:

I hate, I despise your religious feasts; I cannot stand your assemblies. (Amos 5:21)

Stop bringing meaningless offerings! Your incense is detestable to me ... I cannot bear your evil assemblies ... These people honour me with their lips, but their hearts are far from me. They worship me in vain; their teachings are but rules taught by men. (Isaiah 1:13, 29:13)

Woe to you, teachers of the law and Pharisees, you hypocrites! You are like whitewashed tombs, which look beautiful on the outside but on the inside are full of dead mens' bones and everything unclean. (Jesus, in Matthew 23:27)

And they did more than talk. In the single act that scholars agree probably got him crucified, Jesus tried to physically close down the Temple in Jerusalem and end false religion through direct action:

On reaching Jerusalem, Jesus entered the temple area and began driving out those who were buying and selling there. He overturned the tables of the money changers and the benches of those selling doves, and would not allow anyone to carry merchandise through the temple courts. And as he taught them, he said, "My house will be called a house of prayer for all nations. But you have made it a den of robbers." (Mark 11:15-17)

Indeed, Jesus' brief crusade can be seen as an attempt to bring his fellow Jews back to true religion, against the priestly establishment—an effort which caused his murder and ironic transformation into the symbol for the new Pharisees: Christianity.

As Jesus thoroughly points out, Pharisees don't have to examine their own behaviour, or institutions, for they "officially represent" God, and therefore have truth, the law and morality sealed up in unchanging doctrine, and ritual. This feature of religious hierarchies has never changed, any more than has their treatment of those who try to challenge the hierarchy and its orderly "God business". It's also the reason that their power can become absolute and unchallengable.

And yet those who do challenge them, like Jesus, have but a single aim: to bring down the walls that keep some "saved", and others "lost". But the Pharisees must keep those walls up, at any cost. The first seek God in the flesh; the latter keep God under lock and key, to be "dispensed" for the right fee.

It was a joy and an anguish to see this ancient duel break out again and again within my parish in Port Alberni during my years there. It was an inevitable conflict: the civil war between two irreconcilable notions of God and religion that erupts whenever church moves beyond expedient routine into the <u>substance</u> of Jesus' message.

And yet how sad a statement on the United Church, and its spiritual deadness, that this outbreak of Christian truth was perceived by every level of its "leadership" as a threat, to be uprooted and destroyed, rather than a window on the very core of that "Good Trouble" which gives spiritual life, and renewal.

I made the mistake, for quite some time, of thinking that my eviction from such a corpse was some kind of personal loss or defeat for me, when, like the collapse of my loveless marriage, it was a step into authenticity. My "healing", and recovery of a new voice, came to me from elsewhere, and others. And always unexpectedly—as from a long-dead ancestor.

....

Interlude: By Way of a Reflection—On Saints, Ministers, and other Strange Persons

I've been trying to understand what all of this means, in terms of my own faith and spiritual path. An incident helps me with this struggle.

Some months after I was tossed out of St. Andrew's United Church in Port Alberni, I received a rather odd letter from one of the ministers who had done the dirty deed: Foster Freed, who had once been a friend and a classmate of mine during my seminary years. Not letting "friendship" stand in the way of his churchly career advancement, however (in fact, he is now the Chairperson of the entire Presbytery), Foster had been one of the point men in my firing, and had put forward the motion in Presbytery to have me sacked.

His epistle seemed, at first, like the kind of "comfort your victim once you've crucified him" mentality that the church perfected in the residential schools. But as I read it, I realised what a remarkable insight it was into the double-think world of the "successful" minister, who cruises around the commands of the Gospels like a nervous John on Hooker Row, always gawking but never actually <u>doing</u>.

One sentence of Foster's letter seemed to epitomise this paradox:

"Of all of the people I went to seminary with, Kevin, I can safely say that you are the one whose name I would put forward for canonisation. But being a saint, and conducting a successful pastoral ministry, are two different things."

Perfect! What a concise depiction of banality pronouncing judgement, draped in the robes of Constantinian church office; like Pilate before the Mystery.

Actually, reading Foster's confession of his own limitations made me want to cry and laugh at the same time. And yet how strangely similar were his words to the ejaculation of his colleague, Bob Stiven, who declared at my public delisting a year later that I was "pastorally incompetent" for seeking God's will first.

There it was again: that odd counter-posing of God and ministry, right from the horse's mouth (or ass?). But the message is loud and clear, from Foster and Bob and all the other churchly yes-men: in the choice between serving God or the congregation, sorry, but the latter must rule.

Putting the world before heaven—or rather, one's job before one's principles -isn't exactly abnormal, especially in the church, so comments like theirs can be uttered safely, and matter-of-factly, without causing many of us to take offence, or sit up and ask some severe questions. But hearing the crazy truth uttered by Foster and Bob made me realise that their mind-set is really the whole problem, and the cause of all the crimes and suffering I've tried to describe in this book.

I can imagine how, over the past century, the same choice must have presented itself to people like us with a tragic regularity in the residential schools, or at church meetings, where the facts of aboriginal death were becoming known: do I risk scandal, or do I speak out? Does the church remain safe, or does it admit its crime? Always, the same gazing over an unforeseen precipice, the same wondering if faith alone will hold you up. And almost always, the same timid retreat.

What is it like not to draw back, but to step into the void?

That's something the Fosters and the Bobs will never know, which is why they're such good ministers. They and their church have done away with miracles, and acts of faith, for these require steps into the unknown, where vested interest and power politics never tred.

The voyeuristic-glimpses over the edge by such clergy are reserved for prayer and preaching time on Sundays, which is what the crowd wants, and expects, after all; and what their own sense of "clergy self" demands, now and then. But this has nothing at all to do with soaring on the gusts of God, or on the impulses of our true heart, which, like a Galillean storm, can cause a lot of fear if you stay huddled in the boat and refuse the chance to actually walk on the water.

What's it like? I can tell you, because I've been there. It's heaven and hell, all rolled into one. It's that real.

Experiencing what's real is a shock, even to the most brave and daring soul. But once you step off that cliff, you learn so quickly how fanciful and self-serving have been your own views, especially about God; and what happens once you actually take leaps of faith.

First, you fall. No chorus of angels swoops down to save you. There's no crowd of well-wishers on the descent, for you're completely alone. You just keep toppling down, like you see in your nightmares, or on cartoons, with no end in sight. And all you have to cling to is the knowledge of having done the right thing.

Small comfort, that, when you hit bottom.

It's not a soft landing. Every part of you is splattered in a thousand directions.

You spend a lot of time afterwards just collecting all the pieces, and pretending that they will fit together again just like they were before the fall. You may even try making the whole Frankensteinian patchwork work, and walk, and speak again, but it doesn't bear much resemblance to that person who took the plunge.

In the midst of your toil, you notice that you're not alone. A whole crowd of angels and demons—or so they seem to be—has gathered, like spectators in a mud-wrestling match.

Some of these beings keep egging you on—"Get on with things, son! Let's have some closure! Pick yourself up and get a new life!". Others just watch and wait, to see if you collapse for good, laying bets with one another and smiling the whole time, like you're there for their private amusement. Others will stand further away, as if they're afraid of you, with such sadness and yet such joy in their eyes, proud of you, yet contemptuous, too.

But there's something else you realise, after the fall: you're still breathing. And more. The breaths are purer than you've ever known them to be, as if each one is emitted straight from a perfect spring day after the rains have come. Your eyes see through what once was solid rock. And your mind and heart are beating to a new music and presence that makes life before the plunge seem like cardboard cutouts.

You suddenly feel alive, for the very first time.

That's when you realise that you shouldn't try putting your old self back together again. It was splattered for a reason, dummy. Just let all those bloody pieces lie where they are. Something better is emerging, if you have the patience to let it grow.

Love and Death in the Valley

Normally, in the cardboard world of churches and compromises and bartered souls, you wouldn't have the patience and the endurance to wait around for that something better to emerge, amidst the gory remnants that once were you, and your world. But down here, at the roots, everything is possible. The old barriers that your world was based on, which were all in your mind anyway, have been shattered as completely as that old self that stepped off the cliff.

Another novelty is how easily you can step back into the old cardboard world from where you fell, which at first seemed light-years away. It actually co-exists right next to the real world you now inhabit, like a darkened twin. Take a slight turn, and you're back in the shadow-world of the Fosters and the Bobs, where your lesser impulses ruled you like a parasitical little weasel dancing on the head of a sleeping hero, and moving his arms and legs.

The inhabitants of that dark world hate the new you, and scream at you to go away as they squint into your brilliance. And you <u>should</u> leave, too, for you cannot awaken the dozing heroes this side of their own fall.

So I often tell people not to worry about me, and all the splattering I've been through. They should save their concern, instead, for themselves, and all the other denizens of the dark who try to know what's true, and real, within the shadow land of the Fosters and the Bobs.

It's time for the entire sorry mess to take a fall.

....

On February 11th a group of tenants and supporters picketed the head office of the United Church of Canada to protest the activities of two non-profit housing projects, Ecuhome and Keith Witney Homes Society, which are both supported by the church. The Coalition for the Protection of Roomers and Rental Housing sponsored the picket. Tenants in these housing projects are not protected under the Landlord and Tenant Act because Ecuhome and Keith Witney Homes claim they provide rehabilitation and care. One tenant in Ecuhome, who owned a cat, was told to move or get rid of the cat, according to the Coalition. Under the LTA, a person can not be evicted for owning a cat if it does not interfere with others. A woman who lived in Keith Witney was forced to move because she lent her keys to her boyfriend who was doing errands for her when she was sick. Photo by Stuart Mann.

Tenants at Fred Victor Mission Housing picket the
United Church of Canada's head office, Toronto,
February 1993

Love and Death in the Valley

On Sunday morning, August 1, 1999, after the service at Salt Spring United Church, as I was preparing to exit the church, the Reverend Rohanna Laing drew me aside to warn me to "be careful" in my relations with Kevin Annett. She said that she had a friend who was a counsellor or psychologist who knew Kevin. She said that Kevin Annett had "major issues" including "a Jesus complex" and warned me not to get involved with him. I remember that my flags went up regarding her comment because if if the counsellor had done a professional assessment, the resulting information would have been confidential, and acting professionally, the counsellor would not have spoken to Rohanna about it. I responded to Rohanna that "we all have issues. The question is if we can live with each other's issues."

At the time, my sense of Kevin was that he was a man of honesty and integrity. He seemed to me to be stable and truthful, but exhausted after years of severe abuse. Having had daily contact with him since then, I uphold my initial assessment. He is one of the most stable and truthful people I know.

Signed,

Pamela Holm   Date April 19, 2000
Pamela Holm

Chapter Six: An Unfinished Story, or Now What Will You Do?

""Under Third Reich law, the Holocaust was perfectly legal. There was no law, therefore, under which its perpetrators could be prosecuted."

Tina Rosenberg, <u>War Crimes: The Legacy of Nuremburg</u> (1999)

"We don't want money. We don't want power. We want a new world."

Zapatista slogan painted on a wall, Altimarano, Mexico, 1994

Clergy run out of things to say after a few years in the pulpit. Much to the agony of their congregants, their usual response is to become more pedantic and predictable, falling back on the theological "party line" and cliches to get them through their sermons. I haven't met a single colleague who doesn't suffer from this tendency. But in my case, when I ran out of ideas, I opened my pulpit, and let others speak. I couldn't bear the pain and struggle alone.

Besides, as I often said to my parishioners, paraphrasing Woody Allen, "Don't ask me about God. I don't even know how the toaster works."

I've approached this whole, terrible story in much the same manner. I speak from what I know. Whenever I talk publicly about the residential school death camps, or the crimes of church and state in our country, I say what I know, and then rely on those listening to carry it on, however they will. For to continue to speak what I know is true, and have learned, since my firing in 1995 has been the loneliest and most difficult experience of my life, and so it is a burden I have sought to share with whoever will help me.

Very few people want to hear about sterilised children, hidden murders and land thefts by churches in their own backyards. Disbelief and ridicule is their defense against this pain. And for those few who do listen, and are willing to believe that crimes against humanity

Love and Death in the Valley

happen right here in lovely old Canada, the enormity of the crime, and the forces arrayed against them, often saps their resolve and capacity to act. Time and again, this remnant of activists has been struck and scattered by threats and sabotage, and I've found myself alone again with simply the truth to hold onto.

And yet, despite our seemingly lost cause, we are winning, since the truth is on our side, and is provoking change. The criminals and their heirs are beginning to admit that Indian children were experimented on in residential schools under government-funded programs that were run by church doctors. Native activists have voiced the fact of genocide in Canada before United Nations bodies. And the growing hysteria of church leaders over their loss of money to lawsuits from their Indian victims—and the army of knee-jerking media defenders of the supposedly "embattled" churches—is all proving that the tide is beginning to turn.

In fact, a tremendous victory was won on April 27, 2002, when for the first time the stories of witnesses to murder in west coast residential schools were aired on national television in Canada. CTV's "First Story" program interviewed myself and a dozen aboriginal survivors of Catholic and United Church schools, all of whom described atrocities never before mentioned in the media.

Even more encouraging, the United Church publicly caved in over the air. After having denied for years that any crimes went on in their schools, the church's notorious spin doctor, Brian Thorpe, stated on the same program,

"We know that criminal acts occurred in the residential schools ... anything is possible."

My elation on hearing his words was tempered by an amazement, knowing that I had been thrown out of the church and driven into poverty for claiming what Thorpe was now confirming. In their obvious effort to avoid responsibility for their crimes, the United Church has once again ended up merely looking ridiculous: for they would have us believe that one moment, criminal acts never took place in the residential schools, and the next moment, they did!

But, having now admitted in general to the crime, the church and its officials must specifically answer the charges and surrender themselves to justice.

To say that I feel vindicated now is to put it midly. I can see the whole house of Official Lies crumbling before my eyes. But I'm still waiting for a formal apology from the United Church—and from each of the church officials who set out to destroy my work and reputation.

Perhaps this incident illustrates how the tide of truth is inexorable. And yet, a solid barrier still stands against this change, and it resides at the most basic human level: in our personal capacity to disbelieve and deny the truth in front of us.

Admittedly, denying terrible facts is the trait of people who simply do not want to believe them. Bertrand Russell observed, wisely, that if you allege something that affirms a person's belief system, that person will agree with you, even without you providing him a shred of evidence; and conversely, if what you claim contradicts the same person's fixed beliefs, he will deny what you allege, even in the face of flawless proof. This phenomenon is common around the public debate—what there is of it—of Indian residential schools and genocide in Canada.

For example, after I released the evidence showing that thousands of native men, women and children were systematically sterilised at church hospitals in B.C. and Alberta, under federal government programs, the most common and immediate refrain from reporters, church officials and the public was: Where is the proof?

The first-hand testimonies of survivors of these sterilisations isn't enough evidence, it seems, even though such proof was considered "conclusive" at the Nuremburg Trials. And yet, when the mainline churches have alleged, without providing any proof, that they are "going bankrupt" because of residential school lawsuits against them, their claim has been immediately and uncritically repeated across the country, especially on the state-run CBC.

The government and the churches which committed and concealed hideous crimes against humanity in Canada have depended on this "will to disbelieve" in ordinary Canadians as the basis of their continued efforts to avoid answering for these crimes. ***And so it not only behooves each of us to examine our complicity in their efforts, but to do so is actually <u>required</u> under international law.***

Love and Death in the Valley

The Nuremburg Legal Principles, adopted by the United Nations in 1950, <u>require</u> that citizens refuse to support, financially or any other way, institutions which committed or are committing genocide. **Our taxes to Ottawa, and Sunday tithings to the Catholic, Anglican, Presbyterian or United Churches, are violating those Principles, and place us in the same moral category as German citizens under Hitler's Third Reich.**

In addition, an even more solid barrier hinders justice, and continues to protect the criminals and their institutions from prosecution before world courts of justice. That barrier is threefold: the political power of the Canadian government at the United Nations, the psychological power of the Christian churches, and the economic power of the multinational corporations which still require and profit from the extermination of indigenous peoples in Canada and around the world.

This unholy trinity has time and again frustrated the truth from surfacing, and has kept the crimes buried. The church-state-corporate octopus appears to be separate arms only to the observer who doesn't see the whole Beast. In reality, they are limbs of the same Empire, and have worked in tandem to extend European domination over the lands, the resources, and the peoples of this continent. That bloody fact has not changed in five hundred years.

Such domination has not faded with time, but has intensified, as Canadian resources have become all that more vital to the American-based continental bloc that vies with the European Economic Community and the Far East for control of the planet. Aboriginal nations sit astride many of these resources, as do the unmarked graves and other sordid evidence of genocide on countless Indian reserves. It profits the powerful of our continent not at all to disinter this genocide and thereby delegitimate their control of the land. The pale rulers have nothing to gain and everything to lose by genuine aboriginal sovereignty, and the unearthing of mass murder in North America before the United Nations.

The truth, in short, is a huge political liability for the governing elite.

That fact alone has prevented the story and the evidence of the Canadian Holocaust, thus far, from making it on to the agenda at the U.N. and its human rights agencies. It has also cast a veil of silence over our entire investigation in the corporate-run news media, and thereby marginalized the truth to near-oblivion.

Of these three great barriers to change, however, the least obvious and thus more powerful one is the psychological hold Christianity still exerts over many people in the dominant culture, and even among native people. Weyerhauser or the federal government are clear and apparent villains, but the churches are not, even to non-Christians. For they are still viewed as "moral institutions", or religious bodies, rather than the multi-million dollar corporations they in fact have become, run by lawyers and full-time officials.

From this position, the churches can more effectively deceive and engage in wrongdoing than can their business or state counterparts—a fact which has been known, and relied on, for over a century. Indeed, this was the reason that Ottawa gave responsibility for the residential schools to the churches in the first place.

In effect, the Christian churches have served historically as a huge cloak for theft, rape and murder across the planet, and they have never renounced this role. On the contrary; for their role as legitimater of empire has been explicit from the very beginning.

Joseph Conrad put it well in **Heart of Darkness**, when he wrote,

"The conquest of the earth, which mostly means the taking it away from those who have a different complexion or slightly flatter noses than ourselves, is not a pretty thing when you look into it too much. What redeems it is the idea only. An idea at the back of it; not a sentimental pretence but an idea; and an unselfish belief in the idea—something you can set up, and bow down before, and offer a sacrifice to ... ".

We know who and what the "sacrifice" has been. But for our European ancestors, Jesus Christ provided this "idea behind the back" of Genocide, and he still does for our churches. And yet, swimming in the fish tank of our own culture, we aren't aware of this until it's pointed out to us, usually from the outside.

Today, or a century ago, the role of Christianity in conducting and concealing genocide against Indians is analogous to the practice of logging companies which leave a thin stand of cedar trees intact along the highways so that their ecological devastation further inland remains hidden. For not only thousands of lives, but the evidence of this slaughter, has been completely clear-cut by the churches and their accomplices in government. And, as in the Clayoquot rain forest, such destruction is now shielded behind a thin vestige of fabrications which have been left standing to mislead the public, and profit unseen men.

Like hikers in the Clayoquot or Walbran basins, or more accurately like post-war Germans, Canadians need to search past the paltry veneer of constructed truth to discover our own past, and present, treatment of aboriginal peoples—and of other, unnamed victims. The trouble is, we are being sped along the highway past these buried truths so quickly that we aren't allowed to slow down and peer past the Official Lie into the gruesome terrain behind it. The media, the churches, and the various official "opinion makers" in Canada won't allow us a glimpse of the Holocaust that I've tried to share in these pages.

The secrecy, "moral aura" and hierarchical structure of churches made them the ideal institutions to operate the Indian residential schools, since their very legitimacy allowed any kind of atrocity to be performed there with perfect impunity on innocent children, without fear of investigation or exposure. Indeed, so secure has been the image of the churches that even when the truth of the residential school horrors has been revealed, many Canadians simply deny that the churches could have committed such crimes.

This deception carries on today, in the ease with which churches protect and exonerate known criminals in their ranks: like Russell Crossley, a convicted serial rapist in Victoria who worked for more than thirty years as a United Church minister.

Even after he had served eighteen months in prison for serially raping the women in his various congregations, Crossley was officially lauded and honoured by the B.C. Conference of the United Church in 1998 for "his long service as a successful minister" (!). Not only Brian Thorpe, but former Moderators of the United Church and RCMP Superintendents publicly stood by this sexual terrorist, and did so without public protest or comment: the actions of those who <u>know</u> they are above the law.

The United Church has, on paper, a very politically correct position on dealing with sexual abuse and harrassment within the church—just as they had an excellent paper position on native land claims in 1994, which I quoted and relied on when I confronted my Presbytery over its illegal sale of Ahousaht land. But theory and practice must part when vested interests are involved; and when there are criminals and rapists to protect.

Part of the problem in getting Canadians to recognise these Officially Sanctioned crimes is their very enormity, and how they completely implicate the central "establishments" of Euro-Canadian culture: the churches, the government, the RCMP, the judiciary, major corporations, and the medical profession. **The magnitude of genocide in Canada has been the criminals' best defense, for it not only prevents people from grasping, and acting against, these crimes, but it does not create any kind of basis for actually prosecuting the criminals, since they are the people in power.**

As a Victoria reporter told me during the IHRAAM Tribunal in 1998, "This is too huge a story to tell. You're indicting everything Canadians hold dear. Besides which, who's going to bring judges, cops, clergymen and cabinet ministers to justice? Are you going to put the whole system on trial? How?".

Actually, that's <u>precisely</u> what we have to do. Once we know this, the "how?" of doing so becomes much more obvious.

International law and moral opinion is on our side already. So is the evidence, which continues to pour in as more eyewitnesses come forward, now that the naming of killers of native children has become more accepted. But our strongest weapon is the truth, which is like water on a rock-surface: slow but irresistible. And the boulders of lies and violence which have crushed so many survivors of the Canadian Holocaust are beginning to crumble under the constant trickle of the spoken and documented truth.

Of course, seeing things as they are, and speaking about them, is not a good way to "win friends and influence people". Even those who stand to gain by the truth coming out become nervous once you peel back the Official Lies and proclaim publicly that the Emperor, indeed, is as naked as his myths. For the King hates to be exposed, and mocked, and his sword hovers over all of us.

"You sure know how to pick powerful enemies, Kev" laughed Bruce Gunn to me one night during my delisting trial. "MacMillan-Bloedel, the government, the church, the Mounties: shit, who <u>haven't</u> you implicated?".

Ironically, I never set out to expose any of these actors in genocide. If anything, they have tended to implicate themselves by their over-reactions and "preemptive strikes" against those who come close to their crimes. The whole scandal of secret land deals and murdered residential school children blew up for a simple reason: when you bring a candle into a locked room filled with corpses, then death and corruption will be seen for what it is.

The candle, in my case, was not just the open pulpit I instituted at St. Andrew's, or the Loaves and Fishes food bank that first brought native people into church. These were but the candle-holders that held up the light that illuminated the dusky secrets and crimes in the Alberni Valley.

What was that light? I still don't know. It loosened tongues and brought song to sad lives; it fed children and gave me the courage to speak about its miracles to others. But I cannot give it a name.

I owe it everything, and yet it robbed me of all that I knew. Its brilliant blaze caused small souls to scurry like rats for cover, but made others stand up and soar like eagles. It elevated me to a high and holy place, and threw me down from there into deep filth. <u>It forced everyone to make a choice, to see what is</u>. For, whoever was touched by it, the light showed us exactly who and what we are.

"The phenomenal quality of Kevin's services was not so much what happened, as the truthfulness and authenticity about them" commented Jenny Parsons, a chaplain who worked with our "street church" at Fred Victor Mission in Toronto, in 1996. "It became easier for us to know and do God's will during those times. The usual deceptions and platitudes found in churches were completely absent. That made Kevin both loved and hated, since by his preaching and personal example, each of us had to face the demand of the Gospels directly and inescapably."

If that light shone so undiminished during my Port Alberni ministry, it was in part because it was fanned by the winds of necessity. The time had come, quite simply, for the destitute families and stumbling victims of residential school torture to stand up and proclaim their pain and outrage. But they could only do so in a protected space made sacred by their willingness to risk what little they had to force some kind of justice, and change, out of the pale power structure in Port Alberni. These men and women were the ones who transformed St. Andrew's into the beginnings of "a church of the poor".

"This is like our liberated zone" said one of them, Mark Angus, during a church service in 1993. "I feel okay to be myself here and say things that would get me in deep shit anywhere else. We're all equal here, like we are in the eyes of God. I don't have to feel ashamed anymore, or helpless."

It was such empowerment of people on the bottom that definitely had the local power-brokers, like Fred Bishop, nervous, and eventually prompted the coup against our new church. But in the course of this ministry, a different notion of the Christian church was being painfully and slowly created in the Alberni valley: that of a sanctuary and an organizing centre for the victims of the church, of capitalism, and of European culture—**a place from which the oppressed could begin to turn the tables on the powerful**. In short, a practical experiment in Liberation Theology was taking place in our own church, and community.

Ironically, the same United Church that espouses such radical Christianity in <u>other</u> countries, like Nicaragua, reacted like any third world Bishop or dictator when it appeared in Port Alberni: by crushing it as quickly and brutally as possible.

Such is the response of the propertied classes to the "levelling" revolution of the Galileean prophet, and the United Church is certainly more a corporation than a unit in Christ's rebel army. We in his "new church" in Port Alberni knew this, but we could never have imagined the extent to which United Church officers would go to destroy and discredit our efforts to create a church more in line with Jesus himself.

My Mexican friend who was murdered in Chiapas by a death squad, a portly little priest named Javier, shared this same struggle, except the truth of what he and his parish of hungry peasants were up against was obvious for the whole world to see: ruthless landowners backed by the army and gangs of hired killers.

Love and Death in the Valley

Such clarity eludes us in Canada. The very perpetrators of genocide and cover-up pose each day as the new "friends" of native survivors of their Holocaust. On the one hand, the churches destroy dissidents in their own ranks and tribal elders like Earl George who won't play ball, and then posture in the media as the "allies" of oppressed Indians.

Nevertheless, the very absurdity of such posturings by already-indicted criminal bodies, and their spokespeople, is proving their own desperation, and speeding the day when they will stand before international justice. To quote a source within the national office of the United Church, who spoke to me in March of 2001, "It feels like the last days of Richard Nixon around here."

I've spent the years since the 1998 Tribunal trying to counter every new effort by church and state to bury the truth about their ethnic cleansing of Indians. It's been such a ludicrously "hopeless cause" that some days I just laugh about the whole thing. After all, what can I, and a handful of supporters, do when the media, the government, and everybody in between is so willingly collaborating with the churches' campaign to keep thousands of bodies, and the truth, safely interred?

It's all been an incredible test of faith. When the truth is so easily evicted from church, and then beaten up, and left to die in the street unattended, and ridiculed, can it possibly stand up and speak again?

I've learned something I never even sensed when I was a cozy minister, and "faith" was an abstraction: that the truth has a power and movement all of its own, that is—fortunately—not dependent on human efforts, money, media coverage or political power. The simple fact that something **is**—that children were killed and buried in secret, that native land was stolen and sold for profit by Christian churches—begins a counter-motion, like a cyclone gathering strength, against the brutal crimes, lies and cover-ups that seem to rule our "real world".

When we witness to the truth that these things **are**, the cyclone builds that much quicker, taking power from our suffering and sacrifices. But even without us, even if every voice of opposition is stilled and the Official Lies go on, the storm cloud grows, and the counter-motion unsettles what is wrong.

Some say that is because God is behind the cloud, as Judaism teaches, invisible yet guiding all things towards Himself, which is absolute truth and justice. Others, like my atheist friend Joe, attribute this inevitable movement towards rightness to the "banality of evil". To quote Joe,

"It's hard to sustain a lie. It's boring. It takes so much effort to keep doing the wrong thing that everyone gets tired of it after awhile. Even the biggest assholes secretly want the truth to come out. Even they want to do the right thing, except they've forgotten what that is."

That makes a lot of sense to me, but it isn't a very helpful weapon in the daily battle, for wrongdoers—especially the higher up they are—are utterly locked into their behaviour by fear, greed and institutional loyalty. Appealing to them to change on "moral" grounds is worse than naive. Like Teamsters Union leader Jimmy Hoffa liked to say, **"Only when you've got them by their balls do their hearts and minds follow."**

The "balls" of the church, clearly, is money. Only when their property and wealth were threatened by lawsuits did church leaders begin negotiating with their native residential school victims and issuing guarded "apologies", after <u>decades</u> of cover-up and silence.

And not surprisingly. For, as a minister, I have experienced ad nauseam the enslavement of the United Church to that which Jesus called "mammon": the power and riches of this world, and the spirit behind them. Indeed, my experiences at Fred Victor Mission and in Port Alberni have taught me that the United Church is securely in bed with the corporate world, whether that be with logging companies like MacMillan-Bloedel, or in the heart of the beast, not two blocks from Bay street in Toronto's financial district.

What I have been doing since my expulsion from the church seems to be, in one sense, to open the eyes of the world, and church members, to this corporate wolf in churchly clothing. For behind the false image of Christianity the genocide of entire nations has gone on.

This has been a labour of love and death, but mostly of persistence, just like the rainwater which slowly cracks open the heaviest edifice of untruth. I've been blessed with seeing the rock-face of lies and denial begin to crumble, as church and government mandarins admit that, yes, perhaps genocide <u>did</u> happen, and, of course, we <u>did</u> use some native children in medical experiments, long ago. These cracks in the edifice will only widen, and eventually the whole mountain will collapse, despite "all the King's horses, and all the King's men". That's just simple physics, and history.

But, unlike in nature, this process of toppling colossal structures is not automatic; it requires the conscious effort of many people to succeed. Each fissure needs to be exploited with greater pressure— <u>more</u> investigations, <u>more</u> public Tribunals, <u>more</u> demonstrations against the criminals and their guardians in power. For nothing has changed that much since the days of gunboats and residential schools, despite how things appear from the top rungs of our society.

Despite all their public relations spins, bribes, threats and lawyers, and even despite the recent broadcast by the eyewitnesses to murders, the churches which ran the residential schools and the government which set them up <u>have yet to answer any of the charges brought against them by thousands of native people across Canada.</u>

Church and state have deluged us with semi-apologies, regrets, and phony commiserations about the fate of children in their care, but they refuse to answer the charges of murder, sterilisations, and deliberate genocide made against them. When pressed about such avoidance, they attack the questioner, or try to dodge the whole issue by hysterically stoking public fears of "bankrupt churches". **<u>But they still refuse to answer the charges</u>.**

Their intransigence has become even more severe since the release of the 280 page report of The Truth Commission into Genocide in Canada, in February, 2001; the report which I authored, along with numerous native people. Its title sums up the tale: **"<u>Hidden from History: The Canadian Holocaust</u>"**. And its detailed documenting of murder, sterilisations, and torture of generations of innocent children demands a response from the criminals in power, beginning with Prime Minister Jean Chretien, who knew of these crimes as Minister of Indian Affairs during the reign of Prime Minister Trudeau.

A reply is a simple enough thing to do: **<u>Did you or didn't you try to exterminate non-Christian Indians?</u>** But there is only silence to this question—a silence legitimated and echoed by the CBC and other major media across Canada.

King Solomon's Proverbs warn us against expecting justice from institutional authority, since "one official presides over another" in the age-old game of mutual back scratching that keeps criminals protected and lies enthroned. For us to expect that the very institutions which created and maintained the residential schools, and planned the deliberate genocide of generations of Indians, will somehow admit to these crimes, or investigate themselves and put their own officials on trial, would be more crazy than naive.

What is a tragedy can quickly become comedy and farce. The sad spectacle of the RCMP's five year "investigation" into west coast residential schools, which netted a grand total of two prison terms for minor offenders, goes to prove, once again, that when you get Richard Nixon to conduct the Watergate inquiry, the results will always be predictable.

Will the guilty ever confess, when they hold the power? Perhaps it's the wrong question. For it's up to us, the apparently "powerless" majority, to rewrite the terms of power, and history, so that <u>the tables are actually turned</u> on the powerful. That's something Martin Luther King and lots of "ordinary" people have taught me.

Truth isn't our only weapon in this fight. Humour, sarcastically applied to the guilty, is another. It also gets us through the night of despair and keeps us human. When I first picketed the United Church's head office in Vancouver, in December, 1995, what brought the best response, and the most laughs, from passers-by was the placard I carried, quoting George Bernard Shaw: ***"Christianity sounds like a wonderful idea. Somebody should try it sometime."***

Ain't it the truth?

I actually faced down two goons once by getting them to laugh. Honestly. They had just accosted me in the downtown east side of Vancouver one night shortly after the Tribunal, in the summer of 1998, and it seemed curtains-time for old Kev. The absurdity of it all, and perhaps my own fright, caused me to laugh out loud as they grabbed me. That caused them to hesitate, and I said to the biggest one of them, "I bet they aren't even paying you guys very much for this job."

It must have been true, or something, because the big one let go of me and shrugged to his partner. Then the two of them laughed. Maybe they sensed the same absurdity. But it gave me the breathing space to get the hell out of there.

Lots of things, as unforeseen as a sudden radiant break in thunderclouds, can bring us such breathing spaces, and allow us to go on living, and speaking. I've had many such breaks, as have the people who have been able to tell their story to a disbelieving world. We're all survivors.

Merely "surviving", of course, isn't enough. Nor is it an individual effort, when you come down to it. Harriett Nahanee could not have survived as she has without the unseen hands of many. Nor could I have, or the countless survivors of residential school terror. Once you've been steamrollered, you learn that standing with other "victims" isn't just necessary, but your only option.

That's what I'm continuing to do, especially as I finish writing the lines of this book. I'm relying on you, the reader. You are responsible for what you know now, and have learned. You have a responsibility to share the truth and help stand up for what is right. Our future, our very planet, depends on you doing so.

The restless spirits of many thousands of children also depend on you. Their remains lie forgotten in secret burial dumps across our country, where they were shoved quickly one night to hide how they died, and at whose hands.

The murderers of these innocents were never caught, or even named; on the contrary, the murderers were sheltered and aided with praises and cover stories from their churches and government. Criminals like Alfred Caldwell and Dr. George Darby, who sterilised countless native men and women in Bella Bella, were viewed as "honourable men", and died in their beds. **But their victims do not rest. And neither should we.**

In **Soul On Ice**, Eldridge Cleaver says,

"The sins of the fathers are visited upon the heads of the children—but only if the children continue in the evil deeds of the fathers."

Such a judgement is on our heads today, for we are continuing the "evil deeds of the fathers". Ask the aboriginal children who are still sold like cattle to the wealthy pedophiles of the Vancouver Club, if this is not so. Or their cousins on west coast Indian reserves, who live in unheated shacks while their chief and band councillors become rich by selling off ancestral land and timber to multinational corporations. Or every third child in Port Alberni, who goes to bed hungry each night while logging trucks roar out of town, bearing away not only fallen forests, but jobs, and wealth, and a peoples' future.

We live in a closed society in Canada, with no independent media or public watchdog agencies, a state-appointed judiciary riddled with corruption, and a small colonial elite which governs in the interests of foreign corporations and the Americans. In a settler society such as ours, the norms of frontier life still apply, as I learned in Port Alberni: the big landowners run the show, and the rest of us are to keep the secrets quiet when we know of them, and to not ask questions if we don't.

It doesn't always work out that way, of course, and our countryside is strewn with the unmarked graves of those of us, native and pale, who haven't played along with The Game. But their dreams must mingle with the cold reality of the Facts of Death which pose as Polite Society, and Church.

Such love and death bloomed alongside each other for me in the Alberni valley, and often in my dreams I see those same logging trucks carrying away not trees but tiny corpses, and with them the truth. And yet in the same vision I also see what Port Alberni will look like when there are no more food banks, and childrens' limbs are straight again, and the Harriett Nahanees and Fred Bishops are eating together at the same table.

It's a painful yet glorious dream, for it comes out of my own suffering, and those of so many others, including my own children. Clare is becoming a young woman now, and Elinor a boisterous ten year old, and yet in their eyes and tears I see the little girls they were when I was thrown from my church, as I see their deep, present longing for that remote past when we were all one family.

Sometimes, Elinor will look at me with her probing blue eyes and ask me the same question she always has since she was three years old:

"Dad, when are you going to have another church?".

Love and Death in the Valley

There is still such hopefulness in her voice, not only for the reuniting of her parents, and the easing of her own, unnameable pain, but for a return to those times when I took her and Clare on my visits to Indian homes, or to the thundering rapids of the Somass river during spawning time, where hand in hand we watched the bright red sockeye salmon struggle up the falls and mostly suffer and die, so that they could give life.

More than those happy times are gone from our lives. For with them has also vanished something that was alive in the community we were building with such sacrifice in the Alberni valley: a spirit that somehow bridged the two worlds there and allowed inhabitants of each to pass back and forth, and even find a common voice during worship services, or in a food bank line.

I long for the clarity and the flowering of that time, when tired hearts and minds were actually opening. But even if that slice of heaven that somehow fell into our midst of loggers and native families did not survive the closeted ignorance of religion and vested interest, still it beckons to us with the same tugging in our hearts as in my daughter Elinor's.

And perhaps that is the way it will remain, until God or an awakened people come to swing open the doors of our hearts, and of our secret crimes, and make all the rough places smooth, as we are promised. Or, instead, does it fall upon a few of us to not wait for that Coming, but try with our own last drop of self to make the promise real <u>today</u>, by living it as if it was true, now and always? Is such a great and terrible love possible, even when its premature birth brings about our own destruction?

My life says yes, as does Harriett Nahanee's, and many others whose names will never be known. We have stepped from the ashes and made our stand. And yet now, all we have, it seems, is the vision of that brief moment, when we brought God and humanity together in a single thought, and dreamed of justice, even in the valley of death.

For now, we have the vision alone to guide and sustain us. Sometimes, I see it sprout up in the unlikeliest of places and persons, only to get trampled on and uprooted, and then peek up again in some slag heap.

We bleed and die for what is right, we fight for our children and for strangers' children, we are betrayed and crushed down and we rise again, bent and torn but still standing. But we are never complete, and never healed, except in that golden moment and space in which the promise lives, apart from this world of shadow and incompleteness.

Thus do we seem to stumble on as persons "part angel and part devil", in the vision of my hard-line Presbyterian ancestors, or as souls inhabiting two worlds, according to the Gaelic side of my family.

Perhaps I have learned only this: that we make justice happen like we do love—by letting it breathe freely and clearly in our own hearts first, and then having the courage to live it. Thus do flowers bloom in hell.

．．．．．．．．．．．．．．．．．．．．

April 30, 2002
Beltane, The Gaelic New Year—The Time of Birth and Change

Survivors: Kevin Annett and Harriett Nahanee post a list of crimes committed at Indian residential schools on the door of Holy Rosary Roman catholic Church, Vancouver, February 2001

Kevin Annett

Author's Note:

This book should be read in conjunction with my other work, **"Hidden From History: The Canadian Holocaust"**, which is the official report of a six year investigation into crimes of Genocide against native peoples in Canada. It contains the full testimonies of the native survivors of "residential schools" mentioned in this book, along with much archival documentation of our "hidden holocaust".

You can obtain a copy of this 280 page report through the Vancouver Public Library system, or buy your own copy through The Truth Commission into Genocide in Canada, or myself, for $35 (Canadian).

Please help us in our efforts to launch an international War Crimes Tribunal in Canada to prosecute those responsible for the genocide of native peoples, yesterday and today.

Contact myself or The Truth Commission at these numbers:

emails: kevinannett@yahoo.ca
pamela_holm@yahoo.com
websites: http://canadiangenocide.nativeweb.org
http://www.nexusmagazine.com/canada.html
pager (in Canada): 1-888-265-1007
And finally ...

I want to thank each of you who took the time to read my story. In this spirit, let one of my elders have the final word:

"When one man set himself up as the ruler over another, and claimed the earth for himself whilst casting out his neighbour, that was the Fall; but when the earth shall be a common treasury again, with none high or low, and all clerics, priests, teachers, judges and rulers made as common as the rest of us, that shall be the kingdom Christ preached and died for. May the Creator of all people pledge us as one body towards that day."

Gerrard Winstanley, **The True Levellers Creed**, Surrey, England, 1649

About the Author

Reverend Kevin Annett is the author of two books and numerous articles on the genocide of aboriginal peoples in Canada. He is a lecturer in Canadian Studies at Langara College in Vancouver, and holds Masters degrees in Political Science and Theology. Kevin is a regular columnist for the *Republic of East Vancouver* and *The Radical*, and hosts a bi-weekly public affairs program on Vancouver Co-op Radio. His writings have appeared in such international publications as *The New Internationalist*, *Nexus*, *Against The Current* and *Canadian Dimension*.

Kevin is a recipient of the Canada Trust Writers' Achievement Award, and was appointed as the Consultant and Archivist for the first international human rights Tribunal into Indian residential schools, held in Vancouver in June, 1998 by a United Nations affiliate, IHRAAM. He is the pastor of All Peoples' Church in New Westminster, B.C., a multi-faith congregation of native and non-native people.

Printed in Great Britain
by Amazon